The Fallen
& other stories
JOHN MACKENNA

THE
BLACKSTAFF
PRESS

ACKNOWLEDGEMENTS

Some of these stories have already been published: 'Sunday'
and 'Visiting Day' in the *Irish Press*'s 'New Irish Writing',
and 'The Fallen' in *The Second Blackstaff Book of Short Stories*.

First published in 1992 by
The Blackstaff Press Limited
3 Galway Park, Dundonald, Belfast BT16 0AN, Northern Ireland
with the assistance of
The Arts Council of Northern Ireland

Typeset by Textflow Services Limited

Printed by The Guernsey Press Company Limited

British Library Cataloguing in Publication Data
MacKenna, John
Fallen and Other Stories
I. Title
823.914 [FS]
ISBN 0-85640-495-0

for Mary Cunningham
and
Lydia and Ewan MacKenna

CONTENTS

THE UNCLOUDED DAYS

My son drove me home from Dublin tonight. We talked
for a while and then there was nothing to say. Not an uncomfortable silence, just nothing that needed saying and no
need to say anything else. The doctor had nothing much to
say either. Things were under control, he said. Meaning that
things are lying low. That phrase struck me driving between
Kilcullen and Castledermot. The moon had been lying low
and then, quite suddenly, it had climbed high enough to
sweep across the fields at Hobartstown.

'Drive on into Carlow and back the Mill Road,' I asked.

He nodded and we drove past the turn for our house and
out the main Waterford road, on into Carlow and then we
cut back across country and came at the village from a
different direction.

The moon was well up by then and the fields were wintry
pale, even though the night still had summer hanging in the
westerly breeze. Big shadows ballooned from the trunks of
chestnut trees. Not a cloud anywhere on the vast horizon.
Just that magical light in the sky. What I'd have given to
walk out across one of Emerson's fields, my shadow smooth-
ing the ridges and drills before me. I could have done. I
could have said to him to stop the car but I didn't. I sat back
and watched the white light floating by. And then we were
back here, at the house, and I was walking inside and
my daughter-in-law was already wetting tea and my

1

grandchildren were calling from their bedroom and I put the pale fields in the back of my mind because I was glad about this reprieve.

I have cancer of the throat. Not that you'd notice to look at me but it's there, working away like worms under the earth, and when it's ready I'll know, long before the visit to the doctor or the next bout of chemotherapy. I'll know. But for now, for tonight and tomorrow and the rest of this week, I'm still all right.

I'm lying back now in my own bed in my own room in this house I bought in nineteen forty-nine. I live here, with my son and daughter-in-law and my two grandchildren.

They've made great changes to the place, worked hard for what they got. They broke out the back wall, went up a storey, built on three bedrooms and a bathroom. I have my own space. My own room. My own shower. I have privacy when I want it and company when I want it. The grandchildren, they're nine and five, come in and give me kisses goodnight.

I bought this house for the garden. It had grown wild by the time I moved in but I changed so little, I didn't need to. I cut back here and trimmed there and pruned in bits and pieces and, almost overnight, the garden John Wortley had made thirty years before was alive again. The house was secondary and it stayed that way until I married in the summer of nineteen fifty-two. After that the house came back to life.

I still look after that garden. A young chap from the village comes in to do the heavy work, digging and the like, but the rest is left to me. Fruit bushes, fruit trees, vegetables. I do all those. Last summer I put a swing in the branches of one of the plum trees, for the children, and I have a patch of grass at the far end, for them to play ball on, they love that. On fine days I go out there and sit and read the paper. If the throat is up to it, I'll wander down to the gate and talk to people passing by on the road. They used to ask me did I not mind all the changes in the place. I'd say, why would I? There's many a man less sick than I am, many a man younger than I am, ended up in the County Hospital because no one wanted to look after him, I'd say. I'm glad to see the place alive and thriving, I'd say. I waited four years to buy this place and now my son and his wife and my grandchildren are here. That's worth more than keeping things the way they were. No point in looking back.

I was never one for that myself. The odd day I'd sit out in the garden and doze or the occasional night I'd lie here and drift back but not too often. And when I do I think more about the important things that happened than about what I said or did. Mostly. Like, if I was to think back now, I'd say: last year, the Pope's visit; nineteen sixty-three, Kennedy's visit. That's how it would work.

Once in a blue moon I will go back, methodically. The Cuban missile crisis; the Emergency; the constitutional referendum. I lived through that and I can hardly remember a thing about it. I taught it for forty years, forty sets of young fellows and young ones, and it means nothing to me. With the exception of one thing. Summer of nineteen thirty-seven. One person. Alice Moynes. I suppose I was never a government man, never a church man, never even a history man really. More my own man.

3

Or was I? Last Good Friday, I sat out in the garden in the sun. I was just back home from hospital then, the first time in fifty-odd years that I wasn't in the church in that afternoon. I felt I'd won some kind of battle. After all that time. But despite it all – the church-going, the history-teaching, the political nonsense I listened to – I was still my own man. And I got more out of taking the grandchildren to the shop on a Friday, for that white chocolate they like, than I did from the serious business I was supposed to be an expert on.

Lying here, with the moon going down past Prumplestown, I'm happy. To hell with this growth in my throat and the new blocks in the bedroom wall and the fact that next week it might all be different. That doesn't worry me. And tomorrow I'll collect the children at ten past three and we'll walk back here together and I'll have the spuds washed and ready when half past four comes. And that gives me more satisfaction than names and dates and vicious politicians or dead soldiers in pointless ballads. Not that I don't remember anything. I do. Sometimes.

I never saw the point in wearing widow's weeds, dressing in black for all that time. A certain degree of respect, if that is the correct word, a public face on it – yes – but no point in taking the whole thing to extremes. You have your innings and then it's time to carry on and for others to carry on.

Independence is what I've valued most of all. Being able to do what I want to do when it pleases me. I enjoy people. Thoroughly enjoy them. But I enjoy my independence, too. It's something I've savoured from the moment I got it back. But then I was always rebellious, oh not openly so but the strain was always there. I don't know where it came from. Certainly it didn't come from my parents. But it was there, right from the start, running under things.

I was an only child but things were very strict for me. I had madly religious parents. Not that I didn't like them, love them. I did. I was extremely fond of them. But there were things I felt uncomfortable with, from as far back as I can remember. The claustrophobia of the thing. Not the family, of course, but the religious aspects. Not that I even knew, not as a teenage girl, why I felt as I did. It just seemed that as I grew I became more and more aware of the pointlessness of it all, of the religious wall we could neither climb nor break through.

There was the incessant hectoring of people. In the markets and fairs of towns. My father preaching and my mother sitting at a wheezy harmonium, belting out those hymns, some of them bloody awful. Most of them. Oh there were some pleasant ones, good tunes, and I did enjoy singing them. Sometimes I loved singing them. But mostly there was nothing else in the whole farrago for me. I could see that my father was wasting his time. That was a part of it, a frustrating part. My parents, who were so kind to me, to everyone, wasting their time on a pointless exercise. Protestantism, fundamental Protestantism in Ireland in nineteen thirty-seven. Show me anything more ludicrous, more hopeless than that!

I told myself I would never, never get caught on that treadmill of preaching, teaching, singing, standing on wet street corners singing. And what did I do? I ended up on an even worse treadmill of boredom. Sheer bloody boredom. Married to a bank manager who didn't believe life existed

fully beyond the bank counter and, if it did, it was there to
further his banking career. The golf club and the bridge club
were sub-offices for him. Every friend was a potential client
and every social occasion was an opportunity to canvass
business. Oh he was pleasant, witty in a dry way, but there
was always the edge. The ulterior. Not in a cunning way. To
say that would be to be unfair. It was just that he lived for
his work.

God, I hated those golf outings and bridge evenings and
bank dinners and presentation events. I developed the art of
sitting at a bridge table and playing quite well while my
mind was far removed. My first pleasure was in relishing the
fact that the others could have no idea just how far I had
strayed, how totally I had escaped. You can look someone
straight in the eyes, speak to them in an intelligent way,
watch your cards, and yet your mind and body are elsewhere. You can be sixteen and swimming stark naked in a
clear river, somewhere in south Kildare, with the water
lapping the pebbles and your skin touching the water irises
while you're making a perfectly acceptable play in some
smoky hotel dining room. The human mind is a wonderful,
wonderful thing.

You don't remember the name of the river immediately
but you can feel it. Smell it. Oh, the smell of a river bank! You
no longer smell the perfume or the cigar smoke in that room;
you no longer hear their voices. The conversation comes and
goes and you join in but it comes and goes in some remote
place in your mind.

That evening, that place, those people, mean nothing. But
fifty years earlier is as clear and fresh as rain. Moments come

like pictures on one of those modern television screens. Crisp. Clear. Full-coloured. You can reach in there and touch things, feel them.

Occasionally, now, when the river doesn't come, I do find myself back on the streets with my parents. Back on that little box we had, with those religious mottoes on the side. *Jesus is Love. Drink and never thirst again. God loves the Sinner.* I could never remember the other, the fourth. Something about the arms of the Lord. I think.

I was back there the afternoon my husband was buried. All of our friends fussing about the drawing room, offering sandwiches and tea and port. I sat there, having a perfectly coherent conversation and smiling and feeling relieved that I was free again, relishing the thought of the next day and the next and the next and the independence they'd bring. And everyone was talking so quietly and not wanting to upset me and suddenly there I was, back in some village, standing on my little podium, singing as clearly and freely as I ever had.

Lying here, with the moonlight draped across my bed, I believe I could still walk the biggest of Emerson's fields without a trace of tiredness. I used to believe I could do all sorts of things without a problem, even when I was a young lad. I remember arriving for football matches in Castledermot, looking at the big empty field and believing I could easily outrun anybody on the other team and score points from any angle. Time and again I'd believe that. I was the eternal optimist in that regard. It could always be done and I was the one who could do it. I could jump further and higher than I'd done the week before. I was high jumping over a

few branches the day I first met Charlie Donnelly. Now
there's a man I haven't thought of in a long, long time.

That was nineteen thirty-seven. The end of June. I was
working on Emerson's farm for the holidays. My exams
were finished, the end of my second year in University. I was
what, eighteen? Eighteen. It was my third year on Emerson's.
I'd cycled out there the day after I got home from Dublin to
see old Mr Emerson.

'Of course, Martin,' he said. He always said that. Every
year, when I asked about a summer start. I'd been working
there since I was fifteen. I knew all the men out there, they
were friends of my father's, played billiards with him.

'Back for more punishment,' they said when I arrived on
the Monday morning. It was the wettest June anyone could
remember. Emerson's had three new tractors that summer
and they were stuck in the barn. The horses were out again.

I was sent out to one of the outfields to fix up the laths on a
shed, pull down the rotten timber, nail back the loose stuff. I
had the day to myself.

'Bring out your lunch bag, stick at it till it's done,' Mr
Emerson had said. 'You needn't come back in here, just get it
done and then skedaddle.'

It was a bigger job than I'd thought. Best part of a full
day's work but I kept at it. It was good to be inside while the
rain belted down on the tin roof. When the breaks came, I'd
go outside and do what needed doing. I was a conscientious
worker. Maybe that's why I was sent out there. At lunchtime
the sun came out and I pulled down a few branches from a
chestnut and made a rough high jump. I remember tucking
my trousers into my socks, preparing myself for the first

jump and then soaring way over the modest height I'd set myself. I pulled two bales of straw out of the loft and stuck the uprights into those; I was getting more ambitious and I believed, firmly, that I'd crack some kind of record if I kept at it. I was lost in what I was doing and then I heard a shout behind me.

'What a'ya at there?'

This big, grey-haired man in a dirty shirt and rubber boots was standing at the corner of the shed.

'High jumping,' I said.

'Ye'll be for the high jump if Emerson gets ya,' the man said.

I knew that was nonsense but I pulled the branches out of the straw anyway. That was the effect he had on me. Immediately, he sat down on one of the bales and pulled a bottle of tea out of his pocket.

'Sit down and ate yer stuff,' he said.

I sat on the other bale. Two farm workers sitting in the brief sunlight. The man wolfed into his bread.

'Did you start today?' he asked.

'Yes, just this morning.'

'Just this morning. And what's your name?'

'Martin Neill,' I said.

He chewed another mouthful of bread.

'Martin Neill. You must be Paddy Neill's young lad, that works in the beet factory.'

'Yeah,' I said.

The man spat sideways and drank from his tea bottle.

'And what are ya doin' with yerself?'

'I'm in the University, in Dublin,' I said. I suppose I thought he'd be impressed.

'In the University, mind. And what are ya at there?'

'I'm studying history.'

'History bejasus. And do they teach ya anything about tractors there?'

I thought he was joking. I laughed.

'Tractors?'

'Aye tractors.' There wasn't a hint of humour in his voice. 'No, they don't.'

'Did you see the three tractors above in the barn?'

'Yes,' I said.

'Three of the finest tractors in Kildare, locked up in a barn because there's water in the low fields and they're about as useful as a prick on a snowman. That's fuckin' progress for you. That's what the industrial revolution done. Three fuckin' tractors, one more useless nor the other. What do you think of that?'

I remember mumbling, having nothing to say to his tirade.

'I suppose you're right.'

He looked sideways at me.

'Course I'm right.'

Then he chewed on another mouthful of bread. I wished he'd go off and let me get on with the work. There was something about him that was venomous.

'Karl Marx,' he said, when he was finished chewing. 'Now there was a man. *Das Kapital*. That's the book that has it all.'

There was a silence. He was looking at me.

'I never read it,' I said, finally.

'Never read *Das Kapital*,' he roared. 'Never fuckin' read it.'

'It's not on our course.' It was a lame excuse, I knew that as soon as the words were out.

'You never read *Das Kapital*,' he said, ignoring me. 'Not let inside the Catholic University, I s'pose. D'ya see, that's the way of it. The Protestants have the land and the Catholics have their little University and they'll kill one another to hold onto what they have.'

Again the expectant silence, the stare.

'Maybe so.'

'Just fuckin' so, just fuckin' so. And I s'pose you come out here to see how th'other half lives?'

I had him there.

'I've worked here the past three summers.'

'Lookin' in on how the rest of us survive.'

'That's bloody rubbish,' I said.

'And when the nights draw in you'll be off back to Dublin.'

I had him again.

'I have to go back in October, I have no choice.'

But the victory was empty, he ignored what didn't suit him.

'Gettin' fuckin' jumped-up ideas, hah?'

'I've no jumped-up ideas.'

'Like your father. You didn't lick it off the street. Another jumped-up fucker!'

'Fuck off yourself,' I said and I gathered my lunch bag and walked into the shed.

The man stood at the door and roared in after me.

'Why don't you run back up and lick Emerson's arse. You should have plenty of practice. You think you're out of it son, you're out of fuck all.'

I sat in the shed, knowing I was trapped. To walk out would be to face him again. He gathered his bag and his bottle and strolled across the field, making sure I saw him all the way.

That was Charlie Donnelly, though I didn't know his name then. All I knew was what I'd heard and what I could see. The shambling, grey-haired man who had come and gone like an angel of blight.

I remember breaking the chestnut branches into little pieces and flinging them in every direction. I could never take a jump that summer without expecting him behind me. Or so it seemed and yet I haven't thought about him for years, not in this way. Maybe there's something in that.

When I was first diagnosed, when I first heard the news, in that hospital in Dublin, when the word cancer was first mentioned, I remember thinking it didn't sound all that bad. The doctor was reassuring. Treatment. Monitoring. Good general health. Progress. All the phrases rolled out and I felt reassured. Happy almost that I was in such good hands, glad to be of assistance to that man in his chosen vocation. And afterwards, walking down Grafton Street to get a bus to the station, it struck me. I met a woman and, for twenty seconds, I was sure this figure weaving through the crowds was my mother. The image. Dead. But there she was. And even when she passed she still looked familiar. And there was a man beside me in the bus to Heuston, white china skin, who might, for all the world, have been old Mr Emerson when he was laid out.

Ghosts, I thought at the time, coming halfway to meet me.

Thinking about Donnelly this way is a bit the same. Remembering that conversation, if it was the conversation we had. Is that the next step? Now you see us. Now you hear us.

Now you meet us.

If I should die before I wake . . .

That summer, my father decided we were moving out of Dublin. Of course, he discussed it with my mother but he was the one who said to me: I've decided we're moving out of Dublin.

We were travelling on for Jesus.

My uncle, his brother, agreed to take on the running of their printing business himself, at least for the summer. We let our house in Terenure and went West. Well, through Blessington and Naas and Kilcullen. I was accustomed to summer preaching. My parents did it every summer. On the corners of the streets of Dublin. But now that I was finished school, my father said, it was an ideal opportunity to move further afield. To give ourselves a greater commitment.

Preach to the unconverted somewhere in the wilderness between Dublin and Laois, my cousin Lesley said.

It was a wilderness to me but I found the whole thing exciting. Getting away from Dublin. Fields full of flowers, fresh water in the rivers, country roads I could bicycle through. God knew what.

Not that it seemed like that at first. We had an old Ford, everything piled in. And the rain, my God how it rained that June. Staying the first night in Blessington. And then Naas, Kilcullen, Carlow. Creaking stairs; high old beds; the same bedspreads; the rain, everywhere. And all these quaint villages. Moone. My God, how that made me laugh. Timolin; Castledermot; Ballitore; Levitstown; a place called Jerusalem; another called Palatine; Knocknagee.

We stayed in digs while we looked for something more permanent. With families who needed the money but were wary. My father would seethe, quietly, in his room while they prayed the rosary downstairs. My mother would try to mollify him. Once we spent the night sleeping in the car, after he had burst into someone's kitchen and railed about the true path to Jesus. I remember running through the rain while the man in that house told us we'd burn in hell and my father stood in the yard exhorting him to get down on his knees and embrace Jesus.

But we all loved that time. My father relished the challenge. My mother loved the country. I was seventeen. I was free.

We went to look at a cottage in a place called Maganey. My father had decided we would base ourselves in the area. Convert south Kildare, Carlow, Laois, west Wicklow before we moved further afield. It was a battle plan with him. A year and then a decision on whether to continue or retreat to the weekend streets of Dublin.

Maganey was a road off a road off a road, somewhere between Athy and Carlow. The cottage was a small one. Two bedrooms, kitchen, living room. Outside loo across the yard. Corrugated-iron roof. All freshly painted. Neat. A lovely garden full of the most old-fashioned flowers.

We drove out from Carlow with the auctioneer. Passing a public house he said, this is Maganey. A public house and of all things, a station, a railway station. And that was it.

The cottage was almost a mile away, down two roads. The Barrow flowed behind it, three fields distant. The sun was shining on the iron roof, shining after rain. I could see my father reading biblical significance into this shining, burning

14

light. I could almost see the flaming angel of the Lord reflected in his eyes. Somewhere on that roof, close to the chimney, the Guardian Angel had descended and was hovering again, as he had done in Bethlehem. And then it began to rain again.

Inside, we could hardly hear ourselves because of the noise of the rain on the roof.

'Furniture,' the auctioneer shouted. 'Furniture would soak up the sound. Make the world of difference, Mr Moynes. That's all you need. A few chairs and tables, bit of floor-covering and you wouldn't notice a thing!'

And then he stood in the doorway of the kitchen and told us that he knew why we were in the area but his was a policy of live and let live and he bore no ill will to anyone, church or chapel.

'We all have to eat and the place is for renting,' he said. 'Six months or twelve and then an option to buy. That's the situation. No ill will.'

He left us to talk it over and my father smiled.

'It's all money to him,' he said. 'Roman Catholic or Protestant, all solid silver.'

We took the cottage. While we waited for furniture from Dublin, we went on living in digs, travelling from market to market, standing on street corners preaching, giving our tracts to anyone who would take them. My mother pumping the organ; my father perspiring, even on the coolest days; me singing and handing out leaflets. The country was full of competing preachers. There was a general election and a constitutional referendum. I knew nothing of the pros and cons and my father dismissed it as the work of Caesar.

'We're of another King and Kingdom,' he'd say to people. I thought that rather rude. They normally took our tracts without complaint. I'm sure they never read them but they took them.

Once, in Carlow or Tullow or somewhere, when my father had said his piece about that other King and Kingdom, a man caught him by the collar and shouted at him.

'Well why don't you go back to England then, you black bastard.'

Every market was thronged with competition. Politicians and stallholders and ourselves. All of us selling a line on something or other. I could see that clearly. My father couldn't. I think, perhaps, my mother did. We were all there as a form of entertainment for people who had little or nothing else to entertain them.

Once, we stood in the empty Square in Athy, not realising everyone had gone to watch a shop being demolished. It had burned down the night before. It was an endless round. Tuesdays in Castledermot; Wednesdays in Athy; Thursdays in Carlow; Fridays in Tullow. An endless round of rain and noise through that June.

And everywhere the same kinds of people. Small farmers; farm labourers; hucksters; travelling salesmen; conmen; destitute families; children skittering home from school at lunchtime. The same traders doing the same rounds as ourselves. We'd nod and chat to each other. All of us in the same line of business. The regular traders would give us mugs of tea, we'd share our sandwiches.

If the sun shone and we wanted to swim, we'd still be there; if the rain fell, as it did, we'd still turn up. All of us labouring ever onwards. Christian soldiers; soldiers of Mammon. Did it matter a damn? All of us part of the same travelling show.

One of the men on the farm told me Donnelly's name. I didn't ask for any more information. When I got home that evening my father was in the garden.

'God bless the worker,' he said.

I asked him if he'd ever heard of Charlie Donnelly. He leaned on his spade and took his pipe from his pocket. He fiddled with it, the way he always did when he was about to talk about something he disliked.

'Ah yes,' he said. 'Charlie Donnelly. I know him all right. He come up here fornenst Easter time, from Kilkenny direction, and he wasn't a wet week in the place when he come out here one evenin', out here to the house, wantin' me to get him a start in the beet factory.'

I remember the way my father lifted the spade and drove it deeper into the wet clay, making a steadier support to lean on. He had a habit of doing that too. As a child, when someone came to the hedge, I'd know if my father was going to talk for a long time or a short time by the way he drove a spade into the ground.

'No, I'm wrong in that,' he went on. 'He came out demandin' a start in the factory. I told him straight out that it's layin' men off we were, not takin' them on. "As if the fuckin' jobs were yours to give," he says to me and then he starts spewin' out of him like a cesspit. In the end I had to tell him to shag off with himself, in case yer mother heard him. The next thing I know, he's up workin' in Emerson's. I

17

thought Mr Emerson had better sense nor to take on someone like that. But that's him. Why did you ask?'

'No why,' I lied. 'I just met him. I just wondered.'

My father never mentioned him again. But every evening
he'd be there in the garden when I got home. We lived out
beyond Castledermot then, on the Athy road, a place called
Mullaghcreelan. We had a cottage and a cottage acre and my
father would be out there every evening. He made the neat-
est, straightest drills I ever saw.

When I was a small boy, I'd hear him in the garden on
spring mornings at half past five, before he cycled off to
work. I'd wake and the fork would be rasping into the
ground and he'd be whistling and I'd creep over to the
window and pull back the curtain and, as if I was letting
more light in on the garden, he'd always sense that I was
there and he'd turn and wave and I'd wave back and then I'd
pull back the curtains and lie in bed, listening. And the next
thing I'd know was that my mother was calling for me to get
up. I'd look out again and the garden would be empty.

That garden was different from this one. You could see
right across that garden. No trees, no shrubs, plain vegetables with a half-dozen apple trees on the back ditch. If I
looked out this window I'd see shadows and trees and dark-
branched moonlight across the path. This is a complicated
garden. My father's garden was simple. But not my father. I
knew that all along. He was straight and he was as reliable as
a level but he wasn't a simple man. He'd say things that you
wouldn't hear from other men. Like one evening, maybe two
weeks into that summer, he was tricking with me.

'How long are you out in Emerson's now?' he asked.

'A fortnight.'

'A fortnight. And it hasn't stopped rainin' one day. If you're not careful, Mr Emerson'll be blamin' the rain on you and lettin' you go.'

And then he got serious and he leaned across the table.

'D'you know what I miss about not bein' your age again?'

'What?' I said, expecting a smart remark.

'I miss one evenin' like this. After rain. This time of year. I was walkin' along a headland and I brushed agin the corn, green corn, and the smell, the wet, fresh smell that come up off it nearly made me cry. And that same evenin', cyclin' in past the Big Bush it started rainin' and I took shelter under a whitethorn an' the rain come down through it and brought the smell of the May with it. I miss that more nor I miss anythin'.'

I stared at him but there was no mirth in his eyes. He was open to me. I sat there waiting for him to say something else and wishing that he wouldn't. I didn't want that moment broken and still I was afraid he might say something else and I wouldn't know what to do or say. And then he relaxed and took out his pipe again.

'You tell me the tractors is tied up,' he said.

I nodded.

'I suppose yis have the horses out?'

I nodded again.

'Did they set you to tackin' the horses yet?'

I shook my head.

'They wouldn't.'

There was no sense of derision in that remark. It was just a fact.

'That's a skilled job. Not anyone can do it. I remember and I a young lad, twelve or thirteen, I used to go over to Delaney's at the weekend and they'd set me to tackin' the plough horses, big, heavy horses. I'd have to stand on a box to get the tackin' over their heads. Gentle as lambs they were. Isn't it strange, too, the way nature can put the kibosh on progress?'

'How do you mean?'

'Goin' back to the horses. And there's another thing. I see young lads inside with us, in Carlow, young lads your own age, from the town, and they get up in the mornin', get up on their bikes, cycle out to the factory, do the shift, get back on the bikes and cycle home and if you asked one of them to kick a football or run after it even, they couldn't. And they'll tell you that's progress, every man ownin' his own bike!'

He laid his pipes on the table, the pair of them, and took his penknife and cleaners from his waistcoat pocket.

'And these politicians is the same. There's half of them sayin', oh we have to have a new constitution, we have to make changes, go with the times. And the other half sayin' leave well enough alone. And the thing is, the thing is, Martin, that the two lots of them believes completely in what they're sayin'. I don't know.'

I watched him snake the pipecleaner through the shaft, settling himself, now that the rain was down and the garden was out of bounds.

'I'll tell you though, there's one man in this parish that'll see no change and that's the parish priest. I was tellin' your mother. And I comin' home this evenin', cyclin' through

Castledermot, he come out the gate of the parochial house and he flagged me down. "Have you seen any sign of these travellin' preachers?" he says to me. "I haven't, Father," I says. "I heard of them but seen no sign." "They're a danger to the parish," he says. "Are they, Father?" says I, "They are," he says. "And I was wonderin' if yourself and a couple of the other men in the billiard hall might be prepared to do somethin' about them?" Well, I looked at him, Martin, straight in the eye and I said: "Father," I said, "I hope the days of runnin' people out of places and burnin' them for what they believe is well dead and gone." Well, he wasn't one bit pleased, Martin. He turned on his heel and was back up the drive, with the door banged behind him, before I even had time to get me leg over the bar. That's one man that'll see change over his dead body.'

He worked on his pipe quietly and then he looked at me.

'Have you seen any sign of them?'

'No,' I said.

'Ah, well, you won't. Them people now wouldn't want to get their nice clean clothes dirty walkin' across mucky fields. But sure why would they? Unless they're goin' to stand on the walls of the sty and preach to the pigs!'

He chuckled quietly to himself and tapped his pipe on the range door. I can still hear that soft, warm chuckle.

He never came to me, I never saw him on any street after consultations. I saw other people, other men I worked with, teachers I taught with. Often. I dreamed one night that I was in Naas and a bus pulled in beside me and all these people I'd known, people I'd grown up with, got off it. Eight or ten of them, all long dead.

Another time I dreamed I was in a big shop in Dublin, one of those fancy places that smell of heat and perfume, and all the other shoppers were people I'd known who were dead. I remember waking in the hospital and being surprised that I was still alive.

But my father never came to me, never rounded a corner in a crowd or drove past me in a coach full of American tourists and here he is, him and Donnelly, mortal enemies, word for word in my room.

Maybe the doctor was wrong. Or maybe I'll never die. Maybe they're all coming over to see me, to whisper in my head, because I haven't kept my appointment with them on the other side. Wouldn't that be good?

I've never wished for children but had I had a child I should certainly have had two. There are problems being an only child. Certainly in being an only daughter. The closeness of the family was wonderful but it could be lonely. I was not an adult that summer, not in the way my parents were. I envied them their commitment to faith. Occasionally, I doubted my mother's sincerity. Not that she ever said or did anything. It was an intuitive thing on my part. There were moments when she seemed not to be there on the same level of intensity as my father. Not that she could have been. No one could. He was, I suppose, fanatical in some people's eyes. Living so close to him, I didn't see that but I've seen it in other circumstances since. I saw a hint of it in my husband's attitude to business. But that was a different feeling. I was less concerned with it because I found it less interesting. Uninteresting. But with my mother I sensed something, thought I saw something without being able to pin it down. Perhaps my own feelings were hers, blown-up, exaggerated. Fulfilled. Yes, perhaps my doings were the fulfilment of her secrets. But in the day-to-day travelling and preaching there was never a moment I could point to and locate the root of revolt.

Instead, we travelled together and when we arrived in a town we each had our responsibilities. My father would unload the harmonium and set it up; my mother brought out the leaflets and pamphlets and I put out the box with the mottoes.

He always began with a prayer and then we sang. My mother's voice was weak and squeaking. My father's was flat and tuneless. I kept the hymns and songs together. My voice would lift clear of theirs and I especially loved it when I was allowed to sing alone. I loved the performance, the audience, the opportunity to be seen and heard for myself. On those occasions, I was free of whatever hold they had on me and, paradoxically, I was never lonely. That was my medium.

I remember clearly getting back to the cottage one evening and finding a letter from my cousin Lesley in Rathfarnham. She was coming down for the month of July and two weeks in August, she said. I could hardly wait. Living in Dublin, I saw Lesley all the time but, suddenly, her coming down seemed the most promising thing ever.

I could introduce her to the country. To my fields, my roads, my walks, my river. It wasn't that I wanted a position of superiority. It was just an opportunity to share these things with another girl. To say: this is what I've found.

I can still recall the excitement of that evening. Vividly.

My father never mentioned Donnelly to me again. Never. He'd said his piece and there was no more to be said. I had to make my own way from there. Reach my own conclusions.

I'd keep out of Donnelly's way as much as I could. Sometimes in the evenings, when I went down to kick football in the field, he'd be there, sitting on the wall, watching, and the next morning there'd be a gibe.

'Yis couldn't kick shite. The boys down our country'd bate yis before breakfast. Wimmen, oul fuckin' wimmen.'

I did well in keeping clear of him but in the early part of July we were set to cleaning out a scrub wood on the outfarm near Maganey. I cycled out ahead of him and got working immediately. Not because I wanted to but to keep out of his way.

When he arrived, twenty minutes after me, he sat on the ditch and watched me.

'What are ya at?'

'Mr Emerson said we're to stack this timber,' I said.

There were logs and poles on the headland.

'Mr Emerson,' he said, laughing. 'Mr Emerson my arse. Tell me, did anyone ever call you Mr Neill?'

'No,' I said, carrying on with the work.

'No, nor no one ever called me Mr Donnelly. Forty-seven year old and no one ever called me Mr Donnelly.'

He came and stood on the end of a pole I was about to lift.

'And do you know what makes him Mr Emerson? Do ya?'

I said nothing but he went on, as if I wasn't there at all, a cigarette hanging from his lip, jiggling as he spoke.

'Fifteen hundred acres, that's what makes him Mister. Fifteen hundred fuckin' acres. People is afraid of him because he has land. They nod and blink to him wherever he goes. I stood up to the likes of him and I got pissed on and shit on and I learned my lesson. Now I do what they expect.'

He lifted his foot and spat the cigarette into the grass. He walked up to the ditch again and sat down.

'But I know him and his likes for what they are. It's all money, land and power in the end. Emerson and his like have the land and that's their power. The priest and the minister have the pulpit and that's their power. I have nothing but I can shite on the farmer's grass and rub it on his door and I can pull me wire and there's nothin' the priest can do about it. That's my way, boy. I'll take the church shelter of a wet mornin' and the wage packet of a Saturday and fuck them all.'

He stood up again and walked over to where I was stacking logs. He leaned across the timber and looked me straight in the face.

'Never trust them. Education counts for nothin'. They'll savage yer bollocks off if you give them half a chance. They'll shit on you so you shit first.'

His tone was almost intimate and then he spat again and pulled off his coat and set to carrying timber.

When we stopped for tea he asked me whether I'd seen or heard of the travelling preachers. I told him I hadn't.

'They're all the one,' he said. 'Priests, politicians, preachers. Powermongers the whole fuckin' lot of them. They've no time for me but they want my money, my soul, my vote. Whatever little I have they want. But you mark my words, son, put all these Christians in the one ring together and they'll ate one another's arses.'

What was it about Donnelly that made him confide all this in me? Much of it was confidence. He hated my father and he had no time for me but he was prepared to tell me this. Or perhaps I was the only one who'd listen, out of coldness if not interest, without answering back or walking away. I can hear that whispered tone of voice as he leaned across the poles.

'Education counts for nothin'.'

Maybe it was meant to put me in my place but I didn't think so then. It was more of a warning. Or maybe it was both.

I made my parents sit in the car when we got to Maganey station. I was the only one on the platform, waiting, watching for the train that Lesley would come on.

The porter looked out from his office and smiled at me. I smiled back and then walked the length of the platform. The track stretched straight for half a mile towards Carlow. Back towards Athy, the direction from which it would come, it ran straight beneath a bridge and then curved away between trees. I measured my steps the length of the stone walkway singing in time.

All things bright and beautiful, all creatures great and small.
When I turn the train will be in sight. I turned, the track was empty.

All things wise and wonderful, the Lord God made them all.
I shall turn and walk back and then the train will be here.

The purple headed mountain, the river running by,
The sunset and the morning that brightens up the sky.
Oh, when will this train ever arrive.

The cold wind in the winter, the pleasant summer sun,
The ripe fruit in the garden –
There it is, the engine black and massive, the carriages snaking uncertainly, unsteadily behind.

Oh God, I hope she's on it!

And there she was in a waving arm and blowing hair and a shout that was filled with laughter.

Did I ever hear her laugh so much as in that first afternoon? Afterwards, there seemed to be so much of a serious nature to talk about. Of course we laughed again but in between the serious talk of two young women. And later still, Lesley took everything so seriously. Love. Marriage. Money. Home. Living. Death. If I were to say that first afternoon together was an explosion of mirth that preceded a lifetime of longer and longer periods of seriousness, I would be giving it an import that comes from hindsight. But I have often thought about it. We were never as innocent with each other as we were that afternoon when she got off the train. Open, yes. Intimate, yes. Close, yes. But never as laughingly girls again as on that cloudy afternoon – the last cloudy day of that summer.

We stood and hugged and chattered and eventually my father came to take us out to the car. I think he thought we had both fallen under the train but instead he found us gabbling among Lesley's luggage.

It was sometime in that early part of July that the parish priest began to talk about the travelling preachers. I still hadn't seen or heard them. It must have been July because by August we were working Sundays and going down to Levitstown for Mass. We had a dispensation, the weather had been so bad. But the first time I heard him preach about them was in Castledermot, so it must have been July.

I was sitting in the men's short-aisle, I always sat there with my father. It was a strange place to hear a sermon because the pulpit was side-on and the gallery floor cut off any sight of the priest's head. You heard a voice coming out of this pair of shoulders, you saw the hands waving but that was all.

What did he say? He used the stock phrases he always used but he used them with venom. More venom than normal. Yes, yes, he talked about people being attracted, no lured, how could I have forgotten? Lured by the new and the unfamiliar. That was the one weakness of the human character. That Sunday. He began in that quiet way that warned us all of a storm.

There were travelling preachers in the area, going from place to place.

And then the pause and the correction.

No, let us not call them preachers, let us call them what they are. Proselytisers. And these proselytisers are fastening onto the weak, the gullible, the naive.

And then the turn of phrase.

From Baltinglass comes news . . . of a family lured away. A complete family.

And then the punch.

With the exception of one seven-year-old girl, who, having just made her First Holy Communion and filled with the power of the Holy Ghost, said no. No. To the lure. No. To the new. She said no. She is in the care of an aunt while approaches are being made to her family.

And the plan.

These proselytisers have a plan. Of course it is unclear to those of us in the aisles. But the Holy Father has spoken many times of it. He has stressed the need to be wary.

My father gently bumped his knee against mine. I looked at him. A smile flitted across his face.

'This is for me,' he whispered out of the corner of his unmoving mouth.

Those not for the Pope are not for his church.

Those not for the church are not for Christ.

The Devil works in circuitous ways.

'He must,' someone behind us whispers, 'if he bothered with Baltinglass.'

As if he had heard. Could he have? The priest whirls and peers into the men's aisle.

'You men at the back are not listening!'

That desperate silence.

'It is not my job to tell you how to react.'

He turns back to the body of the church.

'You are good people but you cannot allow your faith to be threatened. I will monitor. I will advise. I hope you people are prepared to defend your parish and your faith.'

Is that what he said or is that some composite picked up and stored cynically in the meantime? That or something very like it. A wonderful man to let the last syllable of echo die before continuing. Better nor any preacher or missioner, the people said.

No, I'm being unfair. I couldn't remember that, not the very words. But maybe I'm entitled to that bitterness. It ill becomes me, Father, wherever your shade is now, doesn't it?

You could strike me dead if I wasn't already close to it; stick me to this moonlit floor. But I don't think so.

I don't believe I allowed Lesley the time to unpack her bags before I had her out into the garden, across the gate and into the fields to show her the places and smells and sights I had become familiar with. It seemed that the summer, the real summer we dreamed of annually but rarely got, had arrived off that train.

The next morning the sky was a blue tarpaulin. I took her down to the river where the reeds grew high. I had made a narrow pathway through them to a flat, grass bank. The water was five feet deep. Ideal for swimming. And how pleased I was, too, that here was another real singer. I would no longer have to fight my father's flatness and my mother's squeak alone. I told her about the characters we had come to know at the markets. Not at all like the people in Dublin, much more volatile, much less predictable. I knew Lesley would love them. And I knew my parents were pleased that she had come. They saw her as a surrogate sister for me. They could relax in my regard, at least in the coming weeks.

I took Lesley to see the water irises that first morning, too, on the bend where they grew. All I had ever seen were garden irises. But these were special. We gathered them and brought them back to the cottage. I put a huge jug in our bedroom window, a blue glazed jug, and their yellow flagged heads rose beautifully in the sunlight on the sill. And out beyond them was the corn, turning late and slowly. Lesley would be here for what the local farmers said was the height of the year, the golding of the fields. And day after day there wasn't a cloud anywhere. We would waken at five or six to heat in the room and heat in the garden.

And then I woke one morning, just after five, to the swish sound of a paintbrush on the front wall of the cottage. I got out of bed and walked into the garden. My father was busily whitewashing the wall. But why? It had been bright and white already. And then I saw them, the dark letters through the wet wash. Odd letters, tall, crooked, black. Indecipherable now.

'What did they say?' I asked.

'It doesn't matter,' my father said, smiling.

'This happened during the night. What did they say? You have to tell me.'

My father shrugged and went on whitewashing. My mother came through the door, carrying a cup of tea for him.

I remember turning to her and shouting: 'You have to tell me.' And then I turned back to my father. 'If I'm to be part of what you're doing, if I'm to sing and preach and work with you then you've got to treat me as an equal now. I need to know what it said.'

My father put down the brush and turned to me.

'It said: GO BACK TO DUBBIN,' he laughed.

My mother giggled.

'You think that's funny,' I said. 'All right, it's amusing but it's not funny.'

My mother went on laughing.

'Why would anyone do this?'

'It's happened before,' my mother said. 'Many places. Our

31

first house in Dublin, our car, the organ, walls. You don't think about it.'

'But I don't understand why,' I said, again.

'Anger,' my mother said. 'Blind anger. People hear us and listen and other people are angry with the listeners and we're the ones they vent that anger on. It means nothing. We had a newly painted fence once, a picket fence, at our house in Bray. The night we'd finished painting it, it was daubed. So we painted it again. It was daubed again. We painted it a third time. It was torn down and every stick was broken. In the end it didn't matter. The Lord provides. We'll sing and then we'll eat.'

We sang, the three of us. We stood in the garden and sang and Lesley came and watched from the doorway. Half asleep, she looked at us and laughed. And we all laughed then. I don't remember ever being happier.

We just stood there. No audience. No message. Nothing. Just standing there singing. I believed then, for that moment, that nothing could stop us, that what we were about was correct. And I sang and sang like I'd never done before. I remember the moment, even though the song is gone.

I remember the way the weather took up. Anyone who lived through that summer will remember it. One week we were tramping about in eight inches of mud and a few weeks later there wasn't enough water to go round. The weather lifted like fog, up and was gone. And we were left with days of sun and heat that stretched as tight as a tent from dawn to dusk.

And we were out there working every hour of light that

God sent and beyond. You'd see the dim lights of the tractors dragging up and down the hill fields at all hours. On nights like this, when the moon was full, you wouldn't need lights. Just the chugging out in the countryside and the shadows thrown from the machinery.

We worked shifts those weeks, to catch up with what had been buried by the rain.

I can remember shop assistants stopping on the road at five or six in the morning, on their way home from dances, and shouting at us.

'Go on yis boys yis, quare few wans askin' for yis in Carlow.'

They'd climb onto the ditches and wave till we waved back.

'Get up and ride them maaaaachines!'

By then we'd have been in the field for an hour.

I got home late one night, well after twelve, and found my mother waiting up for me. There was an envelope on the table. It was from the University. I'd passed my exams. I knew I should have been delighted. I was, I suppose, and my mother hugged me and she woke my father to tell him the news, but afterwards, lying in bed, I found it hard to be excited by it. Out there in the fields history meant nothing. It had no place. Its pointlessness, uselessness, was as clear as a ditch when you were out there working in the middle of crops and seasons. I think I lost faith in history from then on. I held onto it, to earn a wage, but no more than that. It was never a living thing again. It wasn't that the moment was of such importance, just the point, the night, where my interest finally ran out. No more than that.

In all my summers on Emerson's, I'd never seen work like we had that summer. I'd be out there in the morning to see people cycling to work; I'd see women on their way intothe town to get the messages; I'd see children straggling along the roads on their way to thin beet; I'd see courting couples walking out the roads after tea; I'd see poachers cutting across the fields in the half-dark and still I'd be there.

I remember stopping the tractor one evening on a headland, getting down for a break. Or do I actually remember this? Have I put it in place? Have the years of putting dates and places on things worked their way into me?

No, I believe I remember this evening.

I stopped the tractor on a headland and got down and I saw two girls crossing the other headland with towels under their arms. I wanted to shout something smart at them but I couldn't think of a word to say and I kept thinking that if Donnelly was here he'd have some smart remark on the tip of his tongue.

Eventually I thought of shouting: I'll be free in two weeks' time if you're interested, but by then it was too late, even if I'd had the courage. They were gone through a gap in the ditch on their way to the river.

I climbed back onto the tractor and carried on working and this bit I do remember clearly. I looked at the sun where it sat in the sky and thought to myself that it must be half past eight and I was delighted that I could feel myself so much at home in the fields that I could tell the time with accuracy and, at the same time, I felt a terrible sense of waste, of time sliding by me, out of my control. I suppose I'm only lucky I don't have that same feeling now.

The wonderful thing about Lesley was that she had no interest whatsoever in religion. Not even a pretence of an interest. She travelled with us, gave out leaflets, sang with us but she thought the whole thing was a complete hoot.

In the evening we would walk down to the river and swim, not another sinner about. When we'd finished in the water we would towel each other's bodies dry. While I towelled her she would tell me about a boy she'd met, from St Columba's, how she would meet him at weekends in Rathfarnham. He was in his final year and that autumn he was going to Trinity to study medicine. She would talk to me in a deep, intimate tone that drew me in to the secrecy of their relationship. I'd find myself sitting closer to catch every breath, every syllable.

She had met him at a Christmas party. He was so beautiful, she said. That was the adjective she used. In anyone else's mouth it would have sounded strange but from Lesley it sounded perfectly natural, correct. She told me his eyes were brown.

'He does all the things you'd want him to do,' she said. 'He listens and he laughs and he treats me like a human being. He doesn't expect me to be foolish or fawning or skittish.'

She told me they'd met every day during the holidays, until she'd had to come down to us. Before that she'd gone up to watch him play cricket at weekends. Seeing him was what she missed most, she said.

One evening she spoke particularly intimately and I remember sitting as still as a stone, waiting for each twist in the tale.

He had taken her, it seemed, in his father's car, to the Sally Gap. They'd gone swimming there, in the rain, without any clothes and afterwards he had dried her down with his shirt and it had been lovely.

'We've been to bed several times since then,' she said.

I caught my breath at the wonder of her frankness, at her daring to do that, to say it.

'I can't wait till he gets his rooms in Trinity,' she said. 'Then we won't have to listen for the sound of his father's car or for his sister.'

God, I envied her. I'm not sure whether it was her boldness or her willingness to tell it all so openly but I envied her.

On evenings like that she'd towel me slowly and show me how he had kissed her and touched her. I was half in love with that boy myself and half in love with Lesley. There was no awkwardness in the things she said or did. I learned so much from her in the most innocent way. No, not innocent, guiltless way. It seemed she was as one with her body as I was with the river. She told me never to accept less from anyone than I was prepared to give.

'There's pleasure on both sides, Alice,' she'd say. 'You know that now. Our mothers would like us to think otherwise and so would a lot of boys I've met, dozens of them. But not now.' And she'd laugh hoarsely. 'Never accept less than you're prepared to give.'

She spent evenings showing me how to kiss, how to touch, how to insist on being myself in search of my own pleasure. All I wanted was to find a spot to bring it all to fruition.

I remember some conversations clearly, some are a blur. But I do remember the sandy spot at the river with the weeds and the rushes growing high. We'd made a narrow entrance so that we couldn't be seen from the field or the road. The river was sunk in weedy banks but the water was clear and deep.

We'd swim and when we'd finished we'd throw our togs in, in case my mother noticed they were dry. We'd throw them in and dive from the bank. I can still feel the rush of coolness from my fingertips, along the rest of my body as it cut through the water. It might be ten o'clock by then, the sun gone down, the night cooling but the water still warm.

Nothing mattered. I loved the days and the singing because they led to the nights and the water and my body at ease in there, at ease in a different world. And then the drying off. Lesley easing the towel about me, caressing me. Everything was perfection. This was how life was meant to be. I'd lie on the bank or sit on the grass and Lesley would embrace me lightly and fondle my breasts and I hers. We would lie together in the twilight, touching so gently at times I was never sure if we had touched.

And then sometimes we would jump into the dark water and I would relish the happiness I had. I imagined that ecstasy was just around the corner. I was convinced of that.

One Sunday in the throes of the harvest we cycled down to Levitstown church. We had a dispensation to work on Sundays, in case the weather broke, and we'd go to Mass in

Levitstown at half past nine because the church was nearer than Castledermot. The parish priest had driven out to say Mass.

I can still remember the dead, stale smell of sweat in that church. Even where we stood, Donnelly and two other men and myself, at the back porch, the smell was heavy and stifling.

He stood for a long time in the pulpit, in silence, letting the importance of his presence sink in and then he began to speak slowly, methodically, he was playing the patient man, the caring shepherd that Sunday.

He allowed us to know a secret, as he often did. Many people had been to see him about the travelling preachers, they were worried. He would tell us what he had told them. He would point us to our faith, our priests, our Pope. He would point us to our God. He reminded us that ours was the one, holy, Catholic and Apostolic church. He refreshed our memories on the oath we took each Easter Saturday when we rejected the Devil and all his works and all his pomps.

'What more can I do?' he asked quietly. 'I am one man. You are the people, the people of God, the people of the church of God.'

I had heard all this before but not what followed.

'You must do, you must do what you think fit in defence of your faith. You must decide and you must . . .'

He let the words hang, I remember, for five seconds, ten, fifteen. People shifted, coughed and still he waited, until the silence was restored. And then he launched his attack. These people had no fear, he said, they had come to the very church gates in Castledermot. They were arrogant, conceited, proud

38

and dangerous. They masked their bitterness in sweet music.

I remember the rest or the gist of it.

'Eve was fooled by such sweetness. Will you be?' He pointed to the front seats.

'Or you?' His finger wandered across the raised faces.

'Or you?' He pointed to the back of the church.

'The people of God must protect the church of God. I cannot do it for you.'

And then that long silence again before he slowly blessed himself and people knelt in their own sweat.

We got away after Communion, pulled our bikes out of the tangle of handlebars at the wall and cycled away from the church, back up towards Kilkea and work. As we pushed up the hill Donnelly pointed to a small, corrugated-iron-roofed cottage.

'That's the so-called den of iniquity,' he laughed. 'That's where them people live. Yer man don't like them preachin' and he don't like them livin' that close to a church and, fuck him, he doesn't want a penny goin' to them. That's the nub of it!'

Donnelly stood up on the pedals of his bike and bellowed back towards the church.

'I'm your priest, you're my people, get out there and kick the shite out of them for me.'

We cycled on, turning left and freewheeling towards Emerson's outfarm.

'Mark my fuckin' words,' Donnelly said. 'I'd like to be in on the kill for this one.'

Was I chilled by what he said? I don't think so. Not then. It meant nothing at the time. I kept clear of him, worked day and night, sweated and pushed and pulled. Did what I was asked. Worked from dawn to well into the darkness. Waited for the last patch of corn to fall.

We finished the harvest on a Saturday morning. I remember sitting on a trailer behind one of the tractors and gate after gate was open from field into field. Everything was cut and dry.

Emerson brought us in for a slap-up feed and then let us go home. As soon as I got back to the house I took a basin out the back and had the first decent wash I'd had in weeks. There hadn't been any point in it up to that. One day's sweat · poured into the next.

The feel and smell of a fresh shirt was a reward in itself. And then up on the bike and into Carlow.

I thought about going to the pictures but I stood in Tullow Street and sucked in the fresh air. My first free night in months. No more hay, no more straw, no more barley, no more wheat, no more tractors, no more trailers, no more work. Too fine to be stuck inside. I wandered around the shops, bought myself a new pair of boots, put them on the carrier of the bike and then I decided to cycle out to Castledermot, up to McEvoy's shop. I'd celebrate. I'd buy myself a bottle of lemonade, maybe two, maybe three!

I remember coming in the Barrack Road, through Prumplestown, past Copes' Mill, pushing the bike as hard as I could. Riding and riding and riding, pushing myself, getting some idea of what it must be like to be a kite. There was a light, warm wind in my face and my hair was blowing back and I bent over the handlebars and stood on the pedals and I began to move faster and faster. I pushed with all the strength I had, bursting my heart and lungs to go as fast as I could and when I could go no faster I sat back, arms out and freewheeled, looking out across the fields on either side. Everything there was cut and dry, too. I closed my eyes for eight seconds and opened them again and shouted across the empty ditches. I was high up in the blue above that road, I was up there flying, soaring on the warmth of air, flying, flying, flying, there was no other word for it. I was that kite in the sky. And I can remember clearly, with a cold accuracy that coming through Carlow Gate, into Castledermot, the kite came down to earth again.

The streets were empty and I thought to myself – where are all the fellows and girls I grew up with? And I knew where they were. Down the River Road or in the Laurels, easy in one another's company and there was I delighted because I had a new pair of boots on the carrier of the bike. I remember slowing to a crawl and thinking what a fool I was for working all year to pass exams and then working all summer to get money to work for another year at more exams. I had five weeks left to get to meet Ann McDonald or Betty Hardy, that was the truth of it.

I pushed on up Athy Street and into the Square and then I stopped. There were these people, a man and a woman and two girls, on the platform beside the pump in the middle of the Square. I stopped the bike and stood watching them. The man was talking about Jesus and then he finished and the woman started playing an organ and they all began singing. I stood there staring at this gorgeous girl with dark hair. I knew there were three or four fellows standing on Copes' corner, smoking, watching me, but I didn't care. I stood there watching and listening and the girl's voice rose free and singing. 'He walks with me and he talks with me.' That's all I can remember of the song, the hymn. Even then I don't think that much sank in.

I'd stayed to watch them pack their bits and pieces into their car. I was in a daze going home. I realised they were the preachers but that was of no importance to me then.

I cycled home that night. Through Hallahoise and down Mullaghcreelan. I lay in bed in the half-darkness and tossed and turned. I thought about getting out the bike and cycling over to where they lived but then I thought better of it.

I remember getting up, opening the window of my bedroom, staring out into the darkness and then lying down again.

I tried to remember the words of the hymn, some phrase of it. It was important to me because I was in love with that girl and her voice was in those words. I was filled with all the passion of a young man. I strained and strained to make contact with the girl. I believed I could, if I only tried hard enough. I held my head between my hands and whispered some imagined phrase into the pillow and the words became hers, the voice was hers. I touched my body with my hands and they became her hands. And afterwards, lying half asleep, I imagined her there. To have someone like that to lie beside me, to wake beside her, to have her there. Just to have her there.

The next morning was Sunday. I was up before anyone else. I was in Castledermot half an hour before Mass began. I hung around outside the church, waiting for them to arrive. In the end, I had to go inside. I stood in the porch, listening, knowing that if I heard one sound of them I'd be gone out of there. I don't think I even waited for my dinner that day. I cycled down through Kilkea, across through Levitstown, down past their cottage. Slowly. The windows were open but the front door was closed and there was no car in the yard. I cycled down to Levitstown Bridge and up again and down again. In the end, I threw my bike across a gate and climbed into the field behind their house. I crept as close as I dared.

The yard at the back of the cottage was empty but for one blue, summer dress hung out on a wire fence to dry. I listened for a long time but there was no sound from the house. I crept closer and stepped across the low wire on the back ditch, crossed the small lawn and stood transfixed. This was the dress the girl had worn in the Square in Castledermot. Did I dare to touch it, to be that close to something so close to her, something so intimate?

I've often thought about that in the times since then and I know there was no decision because there was no choice. I reached out and touched the light material. I forgot about the place I was in, about the chance that someone might come from the cottage, the possibilities of being caught. I touched the cloth but that wasn't enough. I felt its texture but that wasn't enough either. It wasn't the cloth that was important, not even the dress itself. It was what it meant. Whose it was. I took the dress in my hands and buried my face in the warmth of its folds, in the scent of her body, in the folds that folded about her flesh. I was lost in the world of her body.

Of course, sense prevailed or cowardice and I put it back on the wire and recrossed the ditch and went and lay on the

43

hill that overlooked their yard. I lay there watching the house, the yard, the dress. I lay like a stone, watching and listening. I could hear every sound, every wasp, every bird. I could smell the smell of the clover. I strained and strained to be with her. But it wasn't enough for me any more. And nobody came.

A week from the end of that August I began to face the fact that I would soon be alone. Lesley would go back to Rathfarnham and I would come down to that river alone. But I was determined to enjoy every minute of that week.

We went down to swim every evening. The wild flowers were slightly frayed by then – frayed by heat. The sky darkened a little earlier but stayed a constant shade of plunging blue.

We were totally at ease with each other's bodies by then. Not even at ease – easy. We swam and floated and dived and I never felt any need to turn away from Lesley's body or from my own.

We had become aware of a boy watching us from a hill two fields away. He had been there the previous Sunday night and again on the Monday and Tuesday. We laughed about him. As we walked from the cottage to the river we would stop from time to time to watch him. He was too far away to see clearly but we knew he was watching us.

His face seemed as brown as walnut and his shirts were white. As white as snow, as white as May, as white as Queen Anne's lace. I watched him with a particular interest, expectation. I expected, as we swam, that he would come through the weeds but he didn't and I was disappointed.

That Friday afternoon, we drove Lesley to the station at Maganey. The platform was as empty as it had been the evening she arrived. After the train had left I watched it out of sight and then rushed back to the car. I could hardly wait to finish my supper and I was down in the field on my way to the river. And there he was on the hill. I walked particularly slowly.

Come down from your mountain and meet me, I thought.

But the figure stayed there, like Lot's wife, on the hill.

Oh stay there, you may be nothing worth meeting.

I slipped into the water and out again and stood on the bank. I did something I had never done when Lesley was there, I walked to the edge of the weeds and grasses. I knew I could be seen from the road but I could be seen, too, from the hilltop. He must see me.

I stood there, at the edge of the field, and dressed very slowly.

I missed Lesley, of course I missed her, but I felt an excitement. Something was going to happen. I willed it. Something was going to happen. Something was going to happen.

A letter came to our house one afternoon in that first week of September. It was delivered by a young lad on a bicycle. The same letter came to every house in the parish. It was signed by the parish priest. And the Church of Ireland minister. If only I'd kept it. Wouldn't it raise a few eyebrows now? But I can remember the gist of it. I went over it often enough afterwards. It talked about the value of tradition. About people answering different bells but believing in the same Christ.

We'd never heard this kind of talk before. Never.

It talked about two families in Baltinglass and one in Athy being 'led away', that was the phrase that was used. It said the time might soon be ripe for action. But not yet. Approaches were being made to the families. But the time might soon be ripe.

I read the letter when it came and I read it again when my father came home from work and I read it half a dozen times that night but still it had nothing to do with the people I'd seen in Castledermot. These people it talked about had nothing to do with the girl I'd watched dressing on the bank. I sat on the hill that night. Waiting. Sweating.

Of course he was there again the following night. I determined to catch this boy, to confront him. I set out as I always did, went through two gaps in the hedges and, once I was out of his sight, I cut back across the edge of the field, out onto the road and up the back of the hill on which he was sitting.

I ran up that hill and my heart was fluttering with fear. And hope. I remember thinking I was totally insane.

I saw her leaving the cottage, crossing the fields, but she disappeared. I sat waiting, knowing she must reappear but the minutes dragged away and she didn't and the thought struck me that she had finished with swimming. I felt as though my whole life had been leading to this moment and I was faced with emptiness. With nothing. I had never felt a bleakness like that moment. Never.

He was standing on the hilltop when I came up behind him. I thought at every instant he would turn around and see me but he didn't. I had practised, all the way up that hill, what I would say and I said it. Loudly, for all the world as if I was as bold as brass.

'Like David and Bathsheba.'

He started and turned, his face was white beneath the sunburn.

'You frightened me,' he said.

'I thought you were here to watch me,' I said. 'You have been watching me, haven't you?'

He was silent.

'Well haven't you?'

'I saw you in Castledermot, on the Square, singing,' he said.

'You've seen me swimming too,' I said, laughing at his unease. 'I saw you watching me. Do you want to come and swim?'

'I can't swim.'

'Well, walk with me then. Come and keep me company. If you want to.'

He didn't move.

'Perhaps you'd rather sit and watch from here.'

He seemed, at last, to come to life as I turned to walk down the hill.

'No, no, I'll walk with you.'

'Good.'

I took a chance and glanced at him. The paleness was still there beneath the colour. His hair was short and brushed back. His shirt as white as it had seemed from the river bank. He wore scuffed, white canvas shoes. We walked in silence, down the hill and across the field towards the river.

I walked her to the river. She changed into her swimsuit while I sat on the bank, feeling foolish. I watched her turn and dive and roll in the water. It was as if . . . as if she'd been born in that river. Afterwards, she came and sat on the burnt grass and slowly dried her hair.

I sat there, watching and listening.

She asked me if I knew the story of David and Bathsheba. I told her I didn't.

'I thought of it every evening while you were sitting up there,' she said.

I mumbled something.

When she had finished dressing, she asked me if I would walk her home.

We went on walking and walking and I kept expecting her to say goodnight but instead we walked and walked and, before I knew it, I found myself in her parents' house, sitting in their kitchen, talking to her father.

He asked me about University, about my studies, about summer work on the farm, but there was no mention of religion.

I think my parents were pleased to see me with someone for companionship. I imagine they expected Lesley's going would

upset me greatly. I remember my father spoke not a word
about Jesus that evening, not to him. I was so relieved.

He called for me each evening, after that, and we went to
the river. I began teaching him how to swim. In the end, in
desperation, after I'd thought about it a hundred times at
night, I found the courage he never would have and I kissed
him.

After I had done it, I remember feeling a little angry that
everything should have been initiated by me. I told him.

'You should have been the one to do this,' I said.

'Should I?' was all he said.

'You're the one whose close to the land. I'm the preacher's
daughter. I'm not supposed to know anything about this
kind of thing.'

He laughed at that. A wry laugh but it angered me even
more.

'Are you happy just to sit there,' I said, 'and have me come
running to you?'

'I didn't mean it to be like that,' he said.

I shouted at him then. We were sitting in the twilight, on
the river bank.

'You must do what you believe in, that's why my father is
here, that's why I went looking for you, that's why things
happen. Because people make them happen. If you sit up
there on your hill nothing is ever going to happen. You must
know that.'

He was frightened. I could see.

'I didn't know what to do.'

'Of course you did! If you wanted to do something you'd
do it. You do want me, don't you?'

God, I still remember that silence. That awful bloody silence and then my uncertainty. I thought he whispered 'Yes' but I wasn't certain.

'You know what David did when he wanted Bathsheba?' I asked.

He shook his head.

I knew I must tell and tell him in the way I had always seen that story, tell him in every detail. I stood up and looked across the darkening river so that my face was turned from him.

'It happened one evening, when David had risen from his couch and was walking on the roof of his palace, he saw a girl bathing in the river. Her name was Bathsheba. Even from that distance, he fell in love with her. He stood there and watched her bathing and in his mind he wanted her more than anything in his life. It didn't matter that he was married or that she was. He stood there watching her and he knew he must have her. In his heart, he came down from that great height, from his power and his palace, from what people expected of him. He overcame people's ideas and his own doubts and his soul went down to Bathsheba on that river bank. She must have felt the power of his passion surround her and swallow her. She stood there on the bank and she dropped her hair from her fingers and let it roll over her shoulders and David came and took the strands in his fingers and felt for the shape of her face through the hair.'

I turned back towards him then and he was standing directly behind me. He did what I had wanted him to do, he took my face in his hands, felt for the shape of my face through my hair. But I went on talking, I knew I must.

'Once he had done that,' I said, 'once he had broken the barrier that other people saw between them he saw there was no barrier at all. It was as easy as that. And he realised she already sensed what he felt. He felt the strength of her shoulders and knew she could carry whatever weight might fall on them because of what they were about to do.'

He spoke, again in a whisper, but this time I heard.

'And what did they do?'

'She went with him and slept with him. But once they had decided, that became easy. It became as easy as David running his fingers through her hair. As easy as that. My father tells that story as an example of sin but I don't see it that way at all. I see it as a story of passion that would out. I see it as a very beautiful story. It is a very beautiful story, isn't it?'

He said nothing. Instead he kissed my cheek.

'And as true now as then,' I said quietly.

He kissed me again and I opened my lips to his, as Lesley had taught me. We stood there, deep in that one long kiss. My hands were by my side. I slowly reached back and opened the buttons on the back of my dress. His hands slid from my hair and brushed the dress from my shoulders and then he knelt before me, slid down my body, his tongue tracing a course down my throat into the river bed between my breasts. I bent to kiss him and we fell onto the golden grass and I could smell the black river and his clean hair and I could feel the sweat that was his and mine.

The same young fellow who had delivered the letter from the parish priest came two days later to tell me I was wanted in the parochial house. My mother was out at the time and I didn't tell her when she came back. I got out the bicycle and went into Castledermot.

I was left sitting in the parlour for twenty minutes. It smelt of dampness and floor polish.

Twice the housekeeper came in and told me the parish priest was a busy man but I was to wait, I wasn't to go without seeing him. In the end, he arrived.

I stood up and he motioned me to sit down again.

He stood at the window, behind me, looking out across his lawn to the Laurels. He thanked me for coming to see him, congratulated me on passing my examinations, told me I was a bright lad, a lad who had worked hard and made the best of the educational opportunities that had come my way. That was a good thing, he said. A positive thing.

'*Educere*,' he said, 'means the leading out of the potential of the mind.'

How many times did I use that same phrase myself in the years since – and hate myself for it?

'Opening to new ideas,' he said. 'Isn't that what it's all about? And assessing the danger of the new when that danger arises. You're a lucky chap, Martin. Your family has worked hard for you, worked hard to get you where you are. They're working hard to keep you there.'

His tone was warm, understanding.

I found my head falling lower in expectation of the lecture about ingratitude that must follow but he was even better than I'd imagined.

'And the people of the village,' he went on, 'they're proud of you, Martin. In a few years' time, when you're a teacher, they'll say: Martin Neill, yes, I went to school with him, played football with him, I grew up with him and he's a schoolteacher now.'

That respect, he told me, that position brought responsibility. I was at an age where I was beginning to notice girls and that was as it should be. Without that attraction, where would the human race be? And he laughed. He understood these things, just as he understood three, or was it four, years earlier – as if he didn't remember – when he'd given me permission to work on Emerson's farm. The Emersons were a good people, decent people, who recognised religious differences and were prepared to respect them. Live and let live, he said. His voice was deepening, darkening. The storm was upon me.

These proselytisers, he thundered, were a different matter. They lured people, ensnared them.

He appealed to me to be sensible, to think of my career, my faith, my future. Not to risk everything for a few hours in the company of a girl who was being – and I remember this phrase – 'dangled as a lure' before me, being used to trap and ensnare me.

I hardened my hands into fists. If this goes on . . . I thought . . . but his voice became soft again.

'Think, Martin,' he said. 'This is a slippery slope. First your virtue goes, then your faith, then your hope and then everything is gone. Self-respect is lost irretrievably.'

He sighed a deep sigh and walked past me into the hallway and disappeared. I sat there, angry and sweating. Wanting something or someone to attack. I heard footsteps in the hall. The housekeeper.

'He says you're to go,' she said.

There is one incident which I have preserved and taken out into the light of my recollection only occasionally. I have never been sure whether that was because I wanted to ensure its value lasted by not overexamining it, becoming overly familiar with it, or because I found it more daring, more assertive than any other thing we did in our time together. Perhaps it is a little of both.

We had come back one evening from the river to our cottage. My parents were out, visiting someone in Carlow, I think. I took him to my bedroom, to my bed, for the first and only time. We made love, if that is what we did, yes, we made love, quickly, silently, breaths held, listening for my father's car. It must have been quite late because a light shone across the hallway, from the kitchen, into my doorway. It must have been very hot, too, because my window was fully open and I could hear every sound from the roadway. He was so tense. I listened to the cricking of the laburnum pods in the front garden, to the cracking of the roof timbers in the hot darkness. I cupped his seed in my hands to keep it from the white sheets. I poured it slowly onto my skin and rubbed it on my stomach.

I watched him rise and dress and then he watched me.

Another evening we came back from the river, again my parents were away. The front door was daubed with tar. That time it said: DEVIL WORSHIPPERS. When my father returned he helped him clean the tar away. They worked by the light of a storm lamp. I can still see them in the light, standing in their shirt sleeves in the doorway, moths flying about them, scraping off the thick tar. People cycled by in the darkness beyond the light. I remember the sounds of bicycles and then voices falling silent.

People always said they could hear my father's tone of voice in mine. I could never hear it until one evening, a week or so after I'd gone in to see the parish priest.

My father was out in the garden, digging potatoes, when I cycled into the yard. He called me over to look at the potatoes, firm in their bed of clay. I helped him carry a sack of them into the shed and he started talking while we collected the fork and some empty sacks from the garden.

'My job is as safe as houses,' my father said. 'There's nothing that boyo can do to touch it.'

Somehow, I knew he knew about my meeting with the priest.

'He has no say in the beet factory. None,' he went on.

We were standing in the darkness now, in the middle of the half-dug garden. I couldn't see my father's face, just hear his voice, and I began to recognise a turn of phrase, a tone of voice that we shared.

'Oh, I know, I know nothing about this girl. She could be the grandest girl in the country for all I know. I'm not saying she's not. And I'm not telling you not to see her.'

He seemed to be speaking out into the fields, into the trees beyond our back ditch, to someone out there.

'I started out as idealistic as you but I lost it along the way, I lost it because I had to lose it. Just remember in two or three years' time, when you're looking for a teaching job, that's the time this man's words could echo far and wide. But it's up to you. No one can tell you what to do, there's no one can make your mind up for you. You have to look at this from every angle, see it every way and then make your own mind up. Maybe the best thing to do is what you want to do but don't be seen doing it.'

He paused for what seemed a long time and then went on.

'But maybe not. You make up your own mind. Decide yourself. Think it out.'

I wanted to hug him and kiss him and tell him he'd lost nothing. But I didn't. He walked away from me, his big boots were almost silent in the fresh clay.

I knew what I'd do. I'd cycle over the next evening, Wednesday, and wait for her at the cottage. She'd be down with her parents at the station in Maganey, collecting their pamphlets. When she got back we'd cycle over here together. I turned to follow my father inside. He was waiting at the gable of the house.

'If you want to bring her here, if that's what you decide, she'll be welcome. Your mother and myself, like.'

I have often thought since, how rarely I saw the sameness between us. But I did that night. It was a night like this but without a moon. A night when you saw things as straight as a road and as firm.

That evening, when I took him to my bed, is not the only one I hesitate about. There was another which I almost never look at now. Not because it upsets me any more, it did for a long time but not now. Now I look at it with distaste but it has lost its power to frighten me. I am too old to be frightened by it in the way I was when I was seventeen.

It was a Wednesday evening. Once a month, on a Wednesday evening, we drove to Maganey station to collect boxes of pamphlets which came on the late train from Dublin. The porter would have them waiting at the doorway to the platform, my father would tip him and load them into our car.

That Wednesday we drove down as we always did. There were a great number of people in the station yard. Many of them I recognised, men from Castledermot, women and children, too. They seemed to be standing about, aimlessly. My father walked through them towards the door. The boxes of leaflets were there as they always were. My mother and I sat in the car. I noticed the porter staring through the ribbed glass of the ticket office. As my father bent to lift the first of the boxes it seemed as though he was swallowed by the crowd. They swirled about him, shouting, screaming. My mother and I jumped from the car but two men held us back. The crowd was in a frenzy. One man, in particular, I could hear above the others.

'We're a Catholic people,' he was shouting. 'We've had enough of your carry-on. You've stolen enough children from their faith.'

His voice seemed to come first from one part of the crowd and then another, as if he was running about, urging them on. Suddenly he appeared where we were standing, beside the car. He screamed into my face, his mouth inches from mine, spit spattering my face.

'Youse can get yerselves back to hell. Out of here. You'll steal no more children! You hear, none!'

The crowd surged and I knew my father had been knocked to the ground. My mother was crying but I began to scream at this man, at the crowd, at the men holding us.

'Let him go,' I screamed. 'Let him go, you bastards.'

I tried to break free but the man holding me laughed and shouted: 'Shut up, you little fucker. Count yerself lucky.'

And then there was smoke and I realised these people were burning our pamphlets. A woman reached into our car and took my mother's Bible from the seat and it was thrown into the crowd and then onto the fire. My mother and I were bundled back into the car and the crowd opened and I could see the flames dying down. Children were running about, collecting stray leaflets and throwing them onto what remained of the fire. My father came staggering back. His face was ashen. I thought in that moment that he was about to die. He sat into the car and mumbled, 'Christ preserve us all. Bless us.'

The engine started and we began to drive away. A stone clattered on the roof and then another and another and another and another and my mother was weeping.

When I got to their cottage there was no one there. I left my bike in the yard and walked up the field to catch the last of the sun. I was lying out seventy or a hundred yards into the field to get the last of the coppery rays. I must have been half asleep because it was nearly dark and I heard a banging in the yard and the sound of glass breaking. I ran down across the field, over the back ditch and around the side of the house. The front garden seemed to be full of people, men I knew, shopkeepers, farm workers, men from Castledermot.

There were more of them inside the house. The windows had been smashed, the front door kicked off one of its hinges.

I started shouting at them, for all I was worth.

'What are you doing here, for Jesus' sake?'

'Get outta here,' someone said.

I turned to the man nearest me, he was smashing a chair off the front wall.

'Did the priest put you up to this?'

A voice from behind me made me turn, it was Donnelly.

'Fuck off outta that, ya little bollocks.'

'What are you doing here, Donnelly?' I shouted.

'You learn to run with the hare and hunt with the hound, sonny. I always tould ya that.'

'You're a traitor,' I said.

He stood right up to me, his face to mine.

'Safer with the hound boy,' he said and then he smashed his forehead into my cheek, I heard and felt the bone crack and as I was falling his boot crashed into my stomach.

'Now who's a fuckin' traitor, hah? Get outta here if yer not able for it.' He began kicking and kicking and shouting at me. 'Bastard, bastard, bastard, bastard, bastard.'

Every scream was a kick, into the stomach, the face, the testicles, the back. As I rolled under his kicks I saw a man at the window of her room, the room where I'd lain with her. He was bundling clothes through the broken pane. Donnelly picked up one of the blouses and dangled it over me.

'Did ya fuck her, did ya, did ya? Ya did, didn't ya? Ya fucked her.'

He dropped the blouse onto my face and began kicking me again. And then he stopped. There were lights in the yard, a car. The men surged towards it. I heard voices. Warnings. Threats. I turned to see what was happening. The crowd was shouting at the car, at the people, at her parents, at her. She broke through, running towards the house and then she saw me and ran in my direction. Donnelly grabbed her and held her back.

'Go on, fuck her now, go on.'

I thought he was going to kill me. His eyes were burning in the car lights. I began to crawl away, towards the fields, the darkness. He pushed her to the ground and kicked me again. I began to vomit.

He leaned over me.

'The next time it'll be yer fuckin' neck an' yer father's.'

I kept crawling and crawling until I was behind the house, I crawled through the fence wire and stumbled into the field, I ran and ran. I don't know how but I ran and ran up onto the hill.

I could see the house and the yard in the lights from the car.

The crowd seemed to slip away into the darkness. I saw the three figures moving about the yard, collecting clothes, piling them into the car. I knew I had to go down, explain to them that this had nothing to do with me. But I was afraid. I was afraid the crowd would come back. I was afraid of Donnelly. But I had to tell her, explain to her, and then I saw two figures in a gateway a hundred yards down the road, two figures lounging across a gate and I sat on the hill crying. I pressed a cloth against my mouth. A blouse. Her blouse. There was blood on it from my mouth.

I watched them get into the car and drive away.

I sat there for a very long time. For hours. In the end, I
went down to collect my bike. It had been thrown over the
back ditch into the field. By Donnelly, I've always thought. A
last act of kindness to make it easy for me.

I cycled home and hid the blouse under my pillow.

The next evening, when I got back from Naas hospital, my
clothes were all washed and ironed and neatly laid out on
my bed. The blouse was there, too. Washed, ironed, left
unstitched.

I kept that blouse for a long, long time. I told my wife it
belonged to my mother. And then, eventually, it disappeared.

After that evening we went and stayed with my cousins in
Rathfarnham. After the terror, things settled down. My
father went back to his printing business and we moved
back to our house in Terenure. He continued preaching but
stayed in Dublin.

My parents died. I married my bank manager and my
bridge and my golf. Lesley married her doctor. A different
one.

A number of times I travelled to Waterford by train.
Newbridge, Kildare, Athy, Maganey. I often thought about
getting off the train and enquiring.

I could have written. I'm sure a letter would have got to
him. I never did. When I put something behind me I have
done with it.

I sang at my father's funeral and never sang publicly
again. I had done with that, too. It's best in the end.

A SUMMER GIRL

I

Let all bitterness and wrath and anger and clamour and evil speaking be put away from you, with all malice.

Don't ask me for logic, for a straight story, don't fucking ask me for anything like that. Not now. Not when I'm pissed out of my mind. Don't come around here looking for that, none of you. And don't give me that shit about being upset, emotional, in a state of shock. Course I'm in a state of shock but not the one you think. No fucking chance. None. And whatever you do, don't talk to me about the hero he was and how he stood up to this one and that one. Don't give me that shit. None of it. You hear? None of it.

Do you want to know about heroes? Because I can tell you about heroes if you want. I can tell you about kids who were heroes, small kids. Kids that grew up before their time because they had to, because there was no one to do the bringing up for them. They stood, up to their knees in shit because they had to. So don't give me any of this stuff about heroes. I've had it up to here. Right? Had it.

I'll tell you about one. You want someone to put up on an altar to pray to, I'll give you one.

This kid I knew, eleven years old. I was what at the time? Fourteen. Anyway, he lived down the road from us. An ordinary kid. Not the worst, not the best. I'd see him in the shops, at the railway gates, playing football on the green, that kind of thing. He was one of the kids. I wasn't one of the kids by then, I was on my way. Not fucking around yet but on my way to it. Bit here. Bit there. But that's not part of the story. Forget about it.

One time, one Hallowe'en, all of the kids started collecting stuff – tyres, bushes, planks, boxes, all that kind of stuff to make a bonfire. Collecting for weeks before it, piling it up on the green, putting it up and then taking it down and re-arranging the frigging thing. You'd think it was the bloody *Queen Mary* they were building. Everything else came to a standstill – football, conkers, whistling at us. This was the be-all, the end-all, you know. This was life for those two weeks.

Anyway, this kid was right in the thick of it. The Grand Marshal, whatever. Something happened, the day before or the day of the bonfire. Something happened at home, I don't know what. Some trouble he got into. Something. He was grounded. Maybe it was that his parents didn't want him down near the fire. I don't know. Anyway, him and his brother were grounded. They were sent to bed sometime, nine, half nine. The fire was lit at ten. He'd been there for the whole thing so he wasn't going to miss this. Told no one, not even his brother. He was asleep in the other bed in their room. This kid gets out the window about half ten, climbs out onto the garage roof and jumps down and hits the bonfire with the rest of the kids.

No one's quite certain what happened or how. He's there with the rest of them and they're messing around, someone pushes someone and he gets pushed onto the edge of the fire, trousers goes up and his jumper, one of the kids throws a coat over him, puts out the flames and he runs off towards home. The other kids say nothing. It's between him and his parents. He's running, he's all right, he'll get a whipping for destroying his clothes. So what? Anyway, the kid is burned like no one's business, his legs, his back, shoulders, even the back of his head but he says nothing. He's scared, so he says nothing. Climbs up onto the garage roof. Can you imagine the effort it took, the pain? Gets in the window and into bed. He can't get the clothes off, they're burned into him but he says nothing. He doesn't even wake his brother, just gets into bed. Lies there from eleven o'clock until five in the morning when he can't take it any more. He calls his brother and his brother wakes the parents and they shift him to hospital and he hangs on for the rest of the day, until eight that night. And then he dies.

So if you want a hero to put up there, there's one for you. All right? Put a halo on his head. He didn't shout any louder than the rest of the kids, he wasn't always trying to be different. He was just another fucking kid in a small town in Kildare and he had no aspirations to be anything bigger. He just wanted to keep it quiet about what went wrong. That's what I'd call a hero, that's what I'd say. But then he never said anything clever, did he? He didn't get a fucking chance to, did he? He just lay there, saying nothing. As quiet as death. Will he do you? No, he bloody well won't. No chance. But he knew what he should do, didn't he? He knew what he should do. He fucking knew what was right. He knew how to die.

Did you? Did you even know how to live? I'm not talking about you and me, I'm talking about living. Getting on with living. Everywhere you went you dragged that frigging pulpit behind you, that fucking pulpit, you weren't happy when you weren't up there, were you? Or would you admit to it, if you were here? Would one of those other guys tell me it was an altar, that your life was a sacrifice and you were up there for the good of the rest of us, that you never got a kick out of it? They would, wouldn't they? They'd explain it slowly to me because I can't take in anything that doesn't come in between my legs. They'd remind me of things you said. They'd go to a great deal of trouble, wouldn't they? And they'd keep the whisperer away from me because he doesn't think any women can grasp what you were about. We're not up to that. We were only there to cook, to do the washing, keep things presentable. He won't even consider I might have been there for more than that. I might have been there to fuck, mightn't I? But that doesn't enter into the whisperer's picture of things. What does he keep saying? We're all of the flesh. But he doesn't mean it. He means we should all run from our bodies, the way he runs from women, from me.

You didn't run, did you? No fear. You were happy to have us about you. Not that you knew how to treat us. Correction. Not that you knew how to treat me, once we got past the small talk and the public appearances. That's where it all started to fall apart for us, for you and me. When I think of it. When I think of it in the beginning and then I think of the last few weeks. Did it ever strike you, when you hadn't even the time to tell me things, that I was the same woman you couldn't find enough minutes in the day to be with three

65

years back? I remember you telling me that, one evening. Sitting on a wall, one summer evening. You said there wasn't enough minutes in the day to be with me. Too fucking true, sunshine. No time to waste on me. You were too busy being a legend all over the country.

Let me remind you of a night, it could have been any night but this was one particular night. But you won't remember, will you? You're too busy being God now and you were too busy being the next best thing then. Let me tell you anyway.

You remember the blue frock I had. The one you said made me look like the sun on the sea. Fuck, you said that. You came up with that line yourself. Well I wore that the night I'm talking about. I hadn't worn it for six months before that night. It was too cold for wearing it but I wore it anyway. One last big try. It had a tear on the collar but I sewed it so you'd never notice. Not that you would have anyway. But no one would. I spent an hour over that. Not like me. You'd turn the whole thing on its head, if you were here now. You'd say that's what went wrong, that I changed. I started caring. You'd have some half-arsed reason why caring was wrong. But you're not going to make me avoid telling you this. This time you're going to listen. Wherever you are. You're going to listen. Listen to me, fuck you.

I wore this blue frock and I fixed it up so it was right. And I did my hair so it looked good and it smelled clean and you could run your fingers through it and they'd never once snag on a curl. You should've been proud of me. Proud to be seen with me. I was looking better than I ever did. I know I was. I felt it. Fuck you. When I think of it. I remember walking down the stairs and seeing myself in the mirror and thinking, yes I still have it. I can do it. I can dance and I can look smashing and I can get him. I thought you were worth it. And I thought about it walking out of the estate, I didn't care about the coldness of the evening. I knew it was going to be okay. I felt clean.

I thought about guys who used to pay me to come in my hair and I thought to myself – that's done, that's finished with, that's that. And no matter what happens here, it'll never be as bad as that. It'll be okay. What a fool! I thought that was bad. I thought things would never be lower than that again. What a fucking fool.

I remember walking back into the estate with you. Twenty past twelve. You were talking non-stop. Fifty to the dozen. I wasn't even listening. Oh I heard you all right but I wasn't listening. I was thinking about this guy I used to go with, years ago before I got into anything. In Dublin, when I was working there. He was all right. And then one night he called to the house I was staying in. I hadn't seen him for months. It was all fallen apart but he called around. I wasn't there. My sister was. She liked him. I don't mean to fuck. Just liked him. Kept him talking. I was out on the piss with one of the girls from work and the manager of the shop I worked in. They came back with me. I wanted to screw this bloke, the manager. No good reason, just we were all pissed and in the mood for it. I get back, him and this other girl and me. I plant them in the sitting room and I go into the kitchen and there's this other guy with my sister. And he's all serious about me. Wants me to think again, to marry him. Meantime my friend has fallen over asleep in the sitting room and the manager wants to screw me while she's out for the count. And this other bloke is sitting on the stairs with my sister and then she goes off to bed and I'm running in and out from one to the other. In the end, the manager gets fed up, lumps my friend into his car and heads home with her and I get down to screwing the returned Romeo on the couch but I'm too pissed to do it.

Anyway, I was thinking about that, walking back to the house that night. Once. When two guys were interested. Or one, anyway. And you were going on and on about the moral things to do. And I was lying on the stairs with that guy, trying to keep him there and wondering how I could shift the manager from the sitting room. And his hand was inside my shirt and it was as warm and soft as it used to be the first few times I let him touch me. I was back there, lying on the stairs with him. I had it all in front of me then, I kept thinking. And then I remember going into the house with you and throwing my bag on the couch and I knew that was it. It was all pointless. Hopeless. Stupid. I took it all for granted for too long. Not you. I never took you for granted. First, because I wanted you too much. And later on because I could never know what you'd do next. You wouldn't ever let me know from day to day, let alone take you for granted. You bastard.

You gave me this spiel about love that night. About the real meaning of love. You were full of shit. You never knew how to love me. And you never wanted to because you never needed to. Never. Never once. At least that guy that paid me to come in my hair needed that. He needed me for that. He was willing to put his money where his fucking dick was. He needed me for that two minutes. Didn't he? You needed nothing. You never, ever, needed me. Never. Never. Instead you went on with this shit about higher love and important things. You never talked about that in the beginning, did you? Never. When we were dancing and you used to press me against you and you could feel my breasts and my nipples through your shirt and mine, there was no talk about higher love then, was there? Bloody right there wasn't. Not a word. You were happy with that then.

No one could ever say I didn't know how to leave in my time. When it was up I knew and I'd go with some . . . some . . . some fucking grace. I didn't plead with anyone, never. I never got down on my knees to anyone and begged them. And I never filled them full of rubbish about higher things and better things and other lives. I just got my fucking coat or put on my clothes and left. And I'm not talking about customers. I'm talking about guys who weren't paying. I'm talking about love, you know? Not the higher stuff. Nitty gritty, sweaty sex. Having it off. Doing it. I never stayed after the time was up. I just went. But you couldn't even do that. You had to get in a last sermon. In case I didn't appreciate how wonderful you were. In case I thought you were just another bastard who was tired of me. And all that shit about explaining things to me later – did you really think I fell for that? Did you really expect that was washing with me?

Listen, as soon as you kissed me I knew that evening that it was the end. Full stop. I knew it. Once we met at the pub. Just from that one kiss. I knew that was it, gone, sold. And I had to listen to that stuff about how much you'd miss me. You went through the whole thing as if you believed it. Well, I didn't. Not one word. Not one. Once you'd kissed me you were gone, I was gone. You could have saved yourself the next three hours.

Miss me. What were you going to miss? You didn't see me any more. The lights out there were too bright. Every fucking headlamp was a spotlight for you. You thought they were picking you out on the street. You thought people were impressed. You thought I should be content to be seen walking with you one more time.

What were you going to miss? The smell of my hair, the blue frock, the way I laughed, my tits? You weren't going to miss any of it, sunshine. None. I could have taken off my clothes and you'd have seen nothing. You'd have gone on telling me about what the world needed that only you had. Bollocks.

But you were only showing you really loved me, really loved me. Isn't that what the whisperer said to me? More bollocks. Funny way to show it, I said. And he just smiled his crooked little smile.

Do you want to see my tits? I said to him. Do you? For his sake. For the old times. You can.

That stopped his smile. He just walked off.

He was waiting at the cemetery gate.

Don't be angry with me or him, he said to me. It'll do no good. Anger does no good.

I started to unbutton my blouse. Just stood there face to face with him.

Haven't seen him since.

And the funny thing was – that was how long, a week after the last time you were here? – when I got back here after the funeral I was messing about and I found my bag where I'd thrown it on the couch that night we came back here. Whatever sadness was inside my head, if there was any. It went up in smoke. You bastard. You baaaaaaaaaaaaastaaaaaaaard.

I'm fucking better off without you.

II

Teach the young women to be sober, to love their husbands, to love their children, to be discreet, chaste, keepers of the home, good and obedient to their own husbands.

Sometimes I think the reason I don't look out the window any more is for fear of what I might see. Oh, I can walk out the door and go down the street and do things but I never look out that window. Sometimes someone will come in and open the curtains but I'll never look out. I'll wait until night-time to draw them closed again. I'll never close them during the day . . . in case. In case I might look out there and see something I don't want to see. Or maybe, when I think about it, when I really think about, maybe the reason is that I'm afraid of what I mightn't see.

It's like it was with you. It wasn't so much the things you said that made the difference. It was the things you didn't say that were important. That was what told me about how you really felt. Or didn't feel. It doesn't matter.

What I never got to grips with was why you pushed me away. I was often with someone myself, someone that I didn't really want but I wouldn't push them away. And I'm not talking about money. Guys I'd be with. I'd know I'd never be with them again but while I was there I'd never push them away. I'd never do anything to make them think I felt that way about them. I'd never be cruel to them. Never. I never did that to anyone and I couldn't understand why you'd do that to me. Or how. How do you get yourself to being able to do that?

Looking out the window would be like that. Like seeing the gap, the emptiness, like expecting someone to be standing at the gate, counting on it and then just seeing the gateposts and the gate and the street stretching away behind them but with no one in the street. Like having something taken out of you.

It's like a nightmare. Like going into that bedroom. My bedroom. I told you about this and I heard you afterwards using the same story to make some point to a crowd. You did it well, told it better than I did, but you used it without asking me, you told it while I was there, sitting at the back of the room. It sounded like a poem when you told it. It didn't sound that way when I told you. It didn't sound like that at all. When I was listening to you I felt you told it beautifully but I felt angry that you told it. It was my story.

It was true. You made a story of it. It didn't matter whether it was true or not then. You talked about children. About them being the key to everything. But I didn't tell you about children. I told you about a child. One child. One boy. With a name. Pale blue eyes.

I went into the bedroom and he was lying there in his cot with the mobile over it. It was a warm evening, summertime,

about half eight and I opened my blouse to feed him and I
lifted him out of the cot and he was still asleep. He was always
asleep at that time of night. I'd sit at the window with him and
he'd wake up and he'd feed as slow as a snail. He'd take an
hour, an hour and a half, to feed but I didn't care. It was warm
and quiet that time of night. No crowds going up and down
the estate. Just the odd kid whizzing by on her bike or young
fellows going down to the green with a football. I'd sit there
and he'd feed and I'd enjoy it.

I settled him in my arm and put his mouth to my nipple
and still I never noticed. That's the one thing you said to me
when I told you. You must have noticed, you said. But when
you told the story afterwards you said how easy it is not to
notice with children. You used that. But you used it in a
different way. That was a cruel thing to do. Because I didn't
notice until I looked down at him, rumpled up in his Babygro,
until I felt the coldness of his face on my breast, until I saw
the blueness of his mouth. I didn't know until then. And
then I knew only too well. And I knew that once I told
someone else he'd be gone from me for good. The doctor
would take him and then the undertaker and then
the police and then he'd be gone. So I sat there with him, the
same as I would have if he was feeding. I sat there in the
window with him laid against me. And I felt empty and
yet at the same time I felt I was with him for the last time
I'd ever be with him, him and me, and I stayed there
because of that. Until it started to get dark. And then I put
him back down into the cot and I looked at him. His face
was like a cinder. All lined and tired-looking. He was gone.
Changed. I knew it was time to let him go at that stage. I put

on my cardigan and went in next door and asked them to ring for a doctor.

And I told you that story, nearly word for word, and when you told it it had nothing to do with me or that baby, it was your story. And they loved you for it. Women listening to you thought you were so soft, so full of understanding. I just sat there and listened to this strange story about a strange thing that had nothing to do with me. I wasn't particularly angry, not so much that I wanted to jump up and shout that you'd stolen my story. I felt sad. That you took something that dear to me and used it without ever thinking about how I'd feel at losing it, having it taken out of where I'd kept it. It was like you'd taken the baby himself and brought him up there in front of all these people, in front of me, and made use of him to get a point across.

And when I'd think about it, I'd think, no he couldn't have meant it that way, he wouldn't have. And sometimes I was sure you didn't and sometimes I wasn't certain and the odd time I was sure you did. Maybe you never believed me about that baby. Maybe you thought I made it up to get attention. The way you would. Maybe you thought you were taking nothing more than a fucking story from me. Maybe that was it.

But it wasn't just a story.

> Hush little baby . . . don't say a word . . .
> Daddy's gonna buy you a mockingbird . . .
> and if that mockingbird don't sing . . .
> Daddy's gonna buy you a diamond ring . . .

One night, a long time ago, I was driving in from Shannon to Limerick. I was in a car with a fellow, I don't remember who he was. He'd picked me up near the Mills, on the docks, and we drove out the Shannon road, stopped on a lay-by and I did whatever he wanted me to do and he paid me and turfed me out of the car, told me to get the next bus back in from Shannon.

I stood there for twenty minutes and then a bus came along. It was raining, not heavily, just light rain. I flagged the bus down and got in. Paid the driver. It was twenty past ten maybe, maybe half ten, on a Saturday night. There were only two people on the bus apart from the driver and me. These two kids down the back seat. Totally wrapped up in one another. Wrapped around one another. Staring into one another's eyes. Just saying nothing. Staring. Just sitting there in the half-darkness. I couldn't even see their faces that clearly. A car came up behind the bus and I could see their silhouettes. That was as much as I saw of them. I was sitting side-on to them.

I never thought that much about it until one night you and me were coming out of Dublin. Late. On the Naas bus. And there were only three or four people on it and we sat at the back and you had your arm around my shoulder and I remembered the kids on the Limerick bus and I was thrilled because all of a sudden we were them. I didn't tell you about them. It wasn't important to tell you. I knew we were them. I knew how they felt. How I was feeling. How, I supposed, you were feeling. We were sitting there and the bus was driving down the dual carriageway and it was raining and the windows were fogged up and the bus was half dark and no one was talking. Just three or four single figures scattered around the seats up near the front.

It was like being in the pictures. We were looking at these people but they weren't worth watching. We just drifted away from them, back into our own world and forgot about them and about the rain and the bus and the end of the journey and the cold outside. I knew what the kids had felt and I knew I was feeling it. And it was so much better than just imagining it.

I wanted to throw caution to the wind. I wanted you to breathe on my neck. I wanted to feel your breath on my neck. I wanted to feel that warmth, the softness. I didn't ask you, I just pulled your head down slowly until it was resting on my shoulder and I could feel your breathing on my skin, just there, just in the gap between my hair and my jumper. I could feel the regular breathing and that was all I wanted for those few minutes. Nothing more. I was happy just to have that there, to feel that breath, to know you were alive and I was alive. That's all it took to make me happy.

It was that much different the first day I met you. No rain. Sunshine. No bus back seat. I was walking out the road to Athy. It was September. A sunny September evening. I was just walking. Not going anywhere in particular. Just walking for the hell of it, just to get out and enjoy the heat, the fresh air. You were sitting on the side of the road, the motorbike left against a gate. You were just sitting there. Your helmet was on the gatepost and your jacket. You had on a blue tee shirt and blue jeans and leather boots.

You talked to me before I talked to you.

Did you walk all this way out of town? you said.

Yeah, I said, so what?

Nothing, you said. I just wondered. It's a long walk. It's hot. It was hot even on the bike, you said.

Well rest yourself then, I said.

I was being smart, cool, easy with you.

I knew fellows like you well enough.

Maybe you even knew me, I thought, and if you wanted it you could pay for it, like the rest of them.

Anyway, I was older than you. I knew that. Not all that much but enough. Three, four years, I reckoned and I was right there, too.

Sorry, you said.

It sounded like you meant it.

What about you? I said. What are you at?

Just resting, you said.

I can see that. What are you at?

Working in Naas, you said. Furniture place. Thinking about moving. Just took a run down to see this end of the world, you said.

And?

Seen worse.

It's all the one, I said. Wherever you are. There's things to do if you're game for doing them. No matter where you are, you need a thrill. Get it if you want it. Do it if you want to, that's what I say.

You smiled that crooked smile that I used to take for shyness.

I think it was shyness. Then.

Right, you said. What'll thrill you?

Ride on the bike, I said. Get her up to eighty.

I'll try, you said. Here, you said, you put on this jacket.

The helmet won't fit you but put on the jacket, otherwise the wind'll take the clothes off your back.

I held onto you, rounding bends on the grass verge, open roads at eighty or near enough to it, roaring through the country in the quiet evening. The cold came through the jacket. Mixed with the sweat of fear and the heat of the sun. I started to scream and it was half delight and half fear and then you slowed the bike down and slower and slower and slower and we were stopped and I opened my eyes and I thought the world was still spinning past me.

Is that good enough? you said.

I looked out at you, from under the hair that was falling back across my face and I smiled my own crooked, devious smile. But there was nothing bad in it. I just wanted you to know I was grateful. And the two of us stood there beside the bike and neither of us said a word. It got to a stage where I knew neither of us could say anything until something else or someone else broke into the silence.

We were on the side of the road, a straight stretch of road, and there was a church about three hundred yards away and there wasn't a sinner to be seen. Nothing stirring anywhere. Not a sound. And we were just stood there, frozen by the quietness. And the longer it went on the more impossible it got to stir or talk, we were locked into it. I suppose we wanted to touch one another. I did. I wanted to pull you to me or have you pull me to you. I knew there was nothing we could do, not there, not on this stretch of road but I wanted to do something. I wanted to be that close to you that I could feel your skin on mine. I wanted you to feel the sweat on my back, I wanted you to know it was there, to wonder was it

78

the fear of the ride on the bike or the hope of touching you. But I could do nothing about it and it got past the time where you or me could break the silence and make a move. It even started to get dark. The fields started to fade away in a haze of dark blue and light black and we just looked straight out ahead of us, across the road, across the ditch, across the fields, not even daring to look at one another. Afraid we might be caught. I know I was afraid to look at you. Afraid I'd be caught, afraid I'd break something and wouldn't be able to put it together again.

I didn't think of it then but afterwards I thought it was a bit like the evening I sat with the baby, knowing I couldn't break the spell. But this was a different spell. This was hot with sweat and sex. I was waiting for us to touch one another, to be too far gone to care who saw or who said anything. I wanted to be that far gone that nothing outside of us mattered but that passed too and the time just drifted and the mood settled into something different that I can't describe now.

We were just still locked into that and then into the darkness. In the end a car came around the bend and the lights caught us full in the glare so that we couldn't see anyway. We were shaken out of where we were and we had to move, to turn our backs on the light until it passed.

We better go, you said.

Yeah, I said. It's getting chilly.

I'll go slower going back, you said. Just keep in as close to my back as you can.

You'll freeze, I said, in that tee shirt.

No, you said, I'll be all right.

And you drove back really slowly and it seemed to get warmer as we went.

I'd have done anything for you. Anything. And you never wanted me to.

I often heard you say pride was the last thing to go in people. You'd be talking with the others, about people. Or you'd be talking to people and you'd say it. Pride is the last thing to go, you'd say. People cling to pride, they hold it to the end and often beyond, you'd say. They never let it go and if only they did . . . and you'd leave it hang like that. Letting them put their own end to it.

But pride was the first thing to go in me. I'd have done anything for you, I loved you that much. Anything. And you never asked. Because you never wanted.

III

Preaching, to those that perish, is foolishness but to those of us who are saved it is the power of God.

You'd say, tell my side of the story, that's what you'd say, wouldn't you? You always wanted your side of the story told, didn't you? Well once you got into your stride, once you got sure of yourself. Not in the beginning, not the first times I met you but then everyone is on their best behaviour at the start, aren't they? You never meet the real person, not at the start. Never.

I was the keeper of the flame once you began to get into your stride. Isn't that what you told me? The keeper of your flame. I was the keeper. The gaoler. The guard. But it was your flame.

You said not to mind what people said, that they'd talk anyway, that there was no point in paying them any attention. No matter what I say or do, you'd tell me, people will twist and talk about it. I believed you in the beginning. And then I saw through you. And that nonsense. It was just an excuse for you. To do what you wanted to do. I saw it when it came to my door. That's all it was. Rubbish. A way of getting your own way without having to take it head-on. You bastard.

We were driving in a van the day you said that to me, about not caring what people said.

You should know that, you said. What people say is what's inside them, it has nothing to do with you. It's all what's inside them.

Of course I knew but it sounded different. It sounded more certain when it was said like that.

It was a September afternoon. Still sunny, still bright but there was a turn in the air. Things were starting to get colder. We were driving out of Stradbally, towards Athy, and we came on a car in the ditch. It didn't seem that it was too bad, it had skidded in the dry clay into the ditch.

You stopped the van and we got out to see if there was anything we could do. I thought we might have to give them a push back onto the road.

The driver and a woman were standing beside the car.

You asked the man what had happened.

Just skidded on the clay, he said. Just skidded.

The woman turned to us. She was holding a baby. Eight,

ten weeks old. She handed her to me.

She banged against the windscreen, the woman said. I think she's hurt.

I looked at the baby in my arms. I knew straight away.

You came around to our side of the car and looked at the baby.

She's hurt, isn't she? the woman said.

I looked at her and then at the driver. They must know, I thought.

You started talking about life. Everlasting life. You put your hand on the baby, on her face, you ran your fingers down the side of her nose and talked about the life that cannot be quenched, the fire that burns for ever, you said.

I'm not sure whether it was what you were saying or the facts that were sinking in but the woman began to shiver and then to sob and her shoulders began to heave up and down and her head seemed to get lost in the cave between her shoulder blades.

I thought she was going to scream.

Another car stopped and a woman came over to see what was happening.

I think you should take this baby to a hospital, I said.

The woman took the child from me and the baby's mother and the driver followed her and got into the car and she drove away towards Portlaoise.

You stood there and you went on talking, to no one in particular, about life everlasting.

I wanted to scream at you, to tell you stop, to tell you the baby was dead, its neck was broken, but you stood there talking.

I walked back to the van and sat in it, waiting for you. The sun was still shining, I remember, but I felt cold. Partly because of the simple, stupid way the child had died, partly because I was frightened by your coldness, by the way you went on and on when there was no life left. Were you totally cold – did you not realise what you were doing to those people? Of course you didn't, you were too wound up in what you were doing for yourself, in your vision. That was the flame I was to be the keeper of. That was what I was to carry about with me. You thought it was worth keeping.

It was nothing. It was cold. It was hard. It was you and the whisperer. It had nothing for anyone else. Nothing.

I didn't see it so clearly then but I began to see it. I started to understand how the whole thing worked but I was still prepared to listen because I was interested in you. Not in the message or the flame. In you. In your face. Your body. The touch of you. Those were the things I was interested in. The things of the flesh, isn't that what the whisperer would call them? That's what I was interested in. I was prepared to stand near the flame for the sake of being near your body.

I was prepared to listen to you talk to those people and to listen to you talk to knots of people here and there because I wanted to be near you. I couldn't stand the way you talked or some of the things you said. They sounded hollow. They were hollow. But I didn't want to be away from you. I wanted the you that had been silent and hard on the motorcycle. Maybe I thought you'd get back to being that way. I hoped.

I remember going back home one weekend around that time. My mother was horrified. I could see it when she opened the door to me. You're too pale, she said. You're too thin, she said. You're thirty-seven years old, it's time you got yourself in hand, start eating properly, look after yourself, stop running around. You can't behave like a seventeen-year-old at your age and expect to get away with it. Look at you, she said. Wasting away, white as a sheet, look at you.

I said nothing.

I was a great one for saying nothing.

I'd say nothing while I was being fucked, unless I was paid to talk.

I'd say nothing when my mother told me I was wasting away.

I'd say nothing while you were talking to people or while you were telling me I was the keeper of this wonderful flame.

Mostly I'd say nothing at all except when I had to, when I wanted you to make love to me, to touch me, to slide your tongue into my mouth and stop talking and start loving me. Then I'd interrupt. But it got to a stage where you wouldn't even do that. There was no time for that, you'd say. Too much to do, too much to be done. You used to say that as if it was a charm. Too much to do, too much to be done.

When I think back on it I can't understand why I stayed so long. It was just that I never saw myself being used at the time. I never got a clear view of the situation then.

You'd wrap things up in stories. You'd tell stories to people and then you started talking to me in stories.

I remember the last time we travelled together. I had an idea it would be our last journey and I kept thinking back to the first one on your motorbike and wishing myself back there, back then, but there wasn't any way to get back to then or to get you back to the man I thought you were.

Anyway, you started telling me this story about these
people who got money, three or four people, and they went
off and did great things with it, all except one. He buried the
money he was given. When the guy who gave them the
money got back he praised them all for being successful,
except the one who buried his money. You told me the guy
who buried the money was afraid he'd lose it. But the person
who gave him the money took it back and gave it to the
others.

You see, you said, those who work will get there, those
who don't won't. I'm going to spread that word. I want that
kind of person.

But what about the man who did nothing? I asked you.

Out, you said, out of the story. Gone.

But he was afraid, I said.

He's out, you said.

I wanted to tell you something then. That I was afraid.
But I didn't. I haven't told your side of the story, have I? You
wouldn't be satisfied with it. But you told it well enough
yourself. And you could have gone on telling it if you'd
wanted to. Anyway, the whisperer will tell it for you now.

He wouldn't be afraid, would he?

IV

*He sanctified and cleansed us with the washing of the water by
the word.*

I love the woods. I hate the sea. I like the sound of the sea but
I hate the darkness of the water. I always did. Being brought

85

up so far from the sea maybe. In the middle of the woods, on a breezy afternoon, you can lie down, put your hands behind your head and listen to the sound of the leaves and if you close your eyes you could be hearing the sea. The sound without the danger. The whisperer told some people that you died by water because it was a last message to people, to be cleansed by water. That the water washed over you like your words washed over everyone that heard them. He didn't say it to me. He's afraid of me. Me and my tits. You weren't afraid of me.

And I wasn't afraid of you. I was afraid for people near the end. That they'd believe in everything you said. That they'd believe you could bring back their babies, cure their cancer, hold back their pain. I knew you couldn't do that for them and I felt for them. Fuck it, I felt for them when I saw how much they believed. I relied on my heart and I saw that they relied on theirs, they gave you their hearts to be saved from whatever it was they wanted saving from. Sickness. Loneliness. Despair. And you couldn't see that. You could only see your own hands. You couldn't see beyond the hands to the heads that were under them, the limp bodies, the smashed-up fucking hearts that would have done anything to be part of something, part of your circle.

I could look at men that came to you and I could see their lives immediately. I could see them leaving their semi-detached houses in Dublin, their little houses that smelled of emptiness and too much space and I could see them getting into their battered Cortinas in their gardens that were overgrown. I could see them driving like fuck to get to you in Naas or Newbridge or Baltinglass, to hear you, to believe in you, to be cured of something there's no cure for. I could see that, as soon as they came into the hotels. You saw nothing. Fuck you.

I relied on my heart. You relied on your own notions.

I knew.

It wasn't stubbornness. It wasn't that I was a slut and had been fucked by their likes. I just knew what they were going through because I'd been through some of it and I'd heard some of it from their own mouths and I'd had it whispered in my ear when they couldn't come. I'd been in their houses, in their bedrooms that smelled of dirty clothes. Fuck it, I knew them. I could have done more for them. I never ran from them, never ran from anyone. And I won't run from telling you this, not even because you're dead.

I was finished from the minute the others walked into your life. The whisperer, the sloucher and the others. You had them to adore you, to worship at your fucking shrine, hadn't you? I was done for from that minute on. Finished.

I used to lie awake in the last few months, I'd think – if I love him hard enough it'll come back to me. That's bollocks, isn't it? You must've learned at least that when you died. At least that much. You must've learned that. It's a waste of time and energy loving someone that doesn't love you. Love is a fucking waste of time. It won't get you loved if there isn't love on the other side. I could do anything and it'd mean fuck all to you.

I'd make love to you. I never fucked you. You wouldn't hear of that. It was always making love. It had this spiritual thing, didn't it? As if our souls were hanging there over the bed, blessing us in what we did. But you were fucking me, the same as the others did. You just put a polished name on it. Wrapped it up in fancy words. I remember the last time, the second last time we were in bed together. You told me I was a summer girl to you. You didn't say, you're the summer girl and you didn't say, you're my summer girl. You said I was a summer girl. I didn't think too much about it at the time. I wanted you to say the or my but I let it go.

Afterwards I thought about it. A summer girl. Is there a winter girl somewhere or another summer girl? I don't even care any more.

I don't remember how you looked that night. Just what you said. I do remember what you looked like when they took you out at the lock gate. Three days in the water and you looked different. You looked like your skin might break, crack open and spill out something. Not blood or flesh, just spill out something that would pour away and leave you more or less the way you used to be. Your hair looked so much thinner than I remembered, plastered across your porcelain forehead, like a crack on the china that made up your head. And your hands that I loved to touch and be touched by were different, swollen, flabby, white. Where was the colour gone? Did three days in the Barrow wash every ounce of colour out of your body? Did twelve hours of bobbing around in the lock soften every bone in your body?

I found myself wishing you back the way you were, looking the way you used to. I didn't wish you back to life. I didn't feel any loss. It was just for your own sake. I knew how you'd have hated the way you looked. Your strength was gone in the water and it was gone when they lumped you up onto the bank. You were nothing any more. You were nothing to me anyway but you were nothing like the man that made people look into your eyes for hope and health. You were pathetic. A blob of white flesh with water all around you on the dry clay of the bank.

The whisperer never saw you like that. If he did he wouldn't go on with this fucking rubbish about your body being cleansed in the river that weekend. There was nothing magic in that. Nothing. You were a pitiful sight.

But I don't want to talk about you any more or think about you. I want to close my eyes up in the woods. I want to walk up into the woods, where you never walked, and listen to the leaves and maybe not even think about the sea, just listen to the leaves for what they are. And then I want to lie down in the grass and watch the highest parts of the trees and forget I ever knew you.

I want it to be summer again and I want to be a woman out there enjoying the sunshine and not wondering how I can hold you or what people are expecting of you or what you expect of me. I'm happy that the flame went out, well and truly out, in the river.

I wish you could have been the man I thought you were when we were standing in the dark on that road.

Sometime, when I'm lying out in the woods, I'll roll over on my elbow and expect you to be there. But you won't be. You wouldn't have been if you were still here and you certainly won't be now. And then I'll roll onto my back again and look up at the trees. And fuck you.

ABSENT CHILDREN

There was weather that year like no weather I ever remember. From Good Friday on there wasn't a drop of rain and you could count the clouds on the fingers of one hand. Right into the late part of September it stayed clear and hot.

I was working as a painter, a house painter. There was no shortage of work but the weather was the problem. I couldn't spend eight hours a day, five days a week, in the sun. But everyone wanted their house to look immaculate in the good weather. Every white had to be sparkling and every door had to be bright. People go mad at times like that. They expect it's going to last, they think the future is going to be full of sunny days and everything is always going to be as it is at that moment. That's the major problem with the human race – unbounded, groundless optimism.

Still, I wasn't about to turn down work. Even if no one else realised it, I saw the dark days of November when I'd sit looking out at rain and know there wouldn't be another stir of work until the following April.

But I wasn't going to fry for the sake of the money. So I devised a system. I'd get up at four, start at five, work till ten and knock off for the day. Then I'd come back in the evening at six and work till nine. Paint early and paint late was the philosophy. People are impressed when the painter has a philosophy. They reckon they're getting something extra for the money.

90

I was on a run at the time. I'd got five houses on one road. Once the first emerged shining white from four days' work the others began to fall like albino dominoes. It suited me. I didn't have to lug the ladders somewhere new every couple of days and I could buy the paint in bulk and leave it in the yards. Plus, there was the prospect of two or three weeks of watching Mrs Turner. Life wasn't always so kind.

The Turners lived in the second house on the road. I knew that because two days into the first house the bloke who lived there came up on the garage roof and sat there looking down the street at this woman weeding her garden. She was dressed, more or less, in shorts and a bikini top. I'd already seen her myself but this bloke gave me a step-by-step account of how incredible her body was.

When I'd finished work that morning I called to the rest of the houses to see if anyone else wanted work done while I was in the area. That was when the rest of the orders came in. I called to Turner's as well.

A small boy, five or six years old, opened the front door and then went off to find her.

She arrived wearing the same top and another pair of shorts. The bloke in the first house had been conservative in his enthusiasm. I asked her whether she wanted any painting done. She did but she thought her brother was coming to do it for her but would I call back on Wednesday and she could tell me for sure.

Apart from her figure, the most attractive thing about her was her hair. She had a shock of wild brown hair that seemed to explode like an almond firework around her head. When she moved this dance of colour moved in the sun, framing her tanned face and her mouth. In concentrating on her figure, the bloke in the first house had missed what her attractiveness was all about. But who was I to tell him?

I thought about her from the moment I woke on Wednesday morning. I thought about her as I cycled across the Square at five o'clock in the morning. I thought about her as I eyed the blistering paint on the shop fronts, thinking there might be work there after the winter frost got into the cracks. I thought about her as I watched the dust swirl behind my bicycle coming up the road.

In the silence of the morning I pedalled slowly past her house. A tricycle lay on its side on the front lawn. The grass was untrimmed, the side gate left open, the few flowers in the flower bed had given up.

From the top of the ladder, on a street like this, you could always match the garden to the house. The tidy gardens with well-kept flowers and neat tool sheds belonged with the houses I got to work on. The gardens full of blocks and uncut grass belonged with the peeling walls that were left half-painted or never touched at all.

That morning I looked down the line of houses and I knew by the half-finished wall in Turner's back garden that I'd get no work. Her brother would come and paint parts of the house and lose interest and not be seen again for six or seven months.

When I finished at ten, I called to her door. This time she answered herself and asked me to come in, offered me coffee. I sat with her in the kitchen. Straight away she told me her brother was coming to do the job but she'd be interested in buying the paint from me because I'd know how much was needed and I'd be sure to give her something that would last.

I told her that was no problem.

She asked me about myself and I told her as much as I'd want anyone to know. And I told her I thought her hair was smashing.

She laughed.

Well, at least it's my hair you noticed, she said.

It's really nice, I said.

Men tend to comment on other things, she said.

I nodded.

Two days later her brother arrived down to me and I gave him the paint.

Some days I'd see her and she'd wave at me. Other days I didn't see her at all. The following Monday her brother started work, scraping the walls. He did a good job. I stopped to tell him so. Every morning, over the next couple of days, I'd check how he was doing. He was a slow worker but methodical.

Mrs Turner would come and stand in the garden watching him, sometimes. I'd see her from the top of my ladder. I never seemed to see her husband come or go. His car would be there in the morning and again when I'd come back at six but I never saw him.

The following Monday I started on a house across from Turner's. Her brother had obviously worked through the weekend. The ladder was left against the front of the house. About a quarter of the wall had been painted. Three cans of paint sat at the foot of the ladder and a rag was tied loosely around the top rung. I reckoned he should finish the job that day. But he didn't. He didn't come at all and there was no sign of life about the place. Nor the next day nor the next.

On the Thursday, I saw her little boy out cycling his tricycle on the path but still the work stayed undone.

That kind of thing annoyed me. The least he could have done was to start with the front wall and leave the back undone. It was stupid.

When I saw how bloody awful it looked on the Friday morning I was even more pissed off. It wasn't Michelangelo breaking out in me, it was just so pathetic to leave a house looking that way. Why didn't her husband get off his arse and do it?

Still, I thought, I'd leave it to the Monday, see if anyone stirred and if not I'd call on the pretext of seeing what was happening. There might be a half-day's work in finishing it. It wasn't the money but I knew I'd enjoy the view from the ladder if she came out now and then.

Cycling into the street, on the Monday morning, I was praying that the job was still undone. It was. The ladder sat there, the rag still hanging in the early light, the tins untouched.

I worked until ten and then went over. The hall door was open so I tapped on it and called into the hallway. She came from the kitchen. It seemed to take her a moment to realise who I was. I put it down to the sun behind me. Then she smiled but her mouth dropped in a crooked sag that made her look stupid.

I just wondered how the work was going, I said.

She asked me to come in.

I just thought you might like the job finished off, I said. I could run it off in a couple of hours.

Would you? she said.

Of course, I said, if your brother doesn't mind.

He won't be back, she said. His little boy was killed.

Oh, I said.

It came out without my knowing and I could think of nothing else to say.

He cycled his bike out under a lorry, she said. He was ten. Just cycled it out of his gate under a lorry.

I'm sorry to hear that, I said.

And when we went over, the day it happened, she said, his wife was just back from the hospital and she was out on the street, on her knees, washing the tar where he fell. The neighbours had already done it and, anyway, they said there was very little blood. But she was out there with a brush and a basin of water, scrubbing and scrubbing. And the same the morning of the funeral, before we left for the church, she was out scrubbing the roadway. And every day since, my brother said, every day she's out there.

She stopped talking and we both sat there in the sunlit kitchen. She looked different to me. Not that she didn't look as well but this thing threw a different light on her. Hearing this little intimacy had done it. A week earlier I would have treasured any intimacy from her but now that I had heard one it had killed everything. Whatever everything was. Nothing but my imagination. But that was killed, too. I noticed that the twist of her mouth made her look even more stupid and I was angry with myself because I couldn't put my finger on how I felt.

Why should tragedy make this woman seem stupid? There was no logic in what I felt. Was it because it impinged on my fantasy about her? I couldn't explain anything to myself. I only knew that everything had changed in my point of view. That little boy's death and his distraught mother had made this woman look sadly stupid. That had to say something about me. But I couldn't figure what.

I finished her house that morning. I worked on into the midday heat and got it finished. I laid the ladder and the cans at the side of the house and left without saying anything.

I was back at half past four the following morning and I'd finished the last of my houses by nine.

I brought up the van and put the ladders, brushes, paints and covers away. I was gone by ten, before her door was even opened. I never really thought of her again. I thought of me and her, me and the way I'd changed in looking at her and what perplexed, perplexes, most is the fact that I cannot define what happened. That frightens me. I changed inside in that moment in my way of seeing her and for no good reason other than her grief. That must say something, something terrifying, about me but the worst part is that I don't know what.

SUNDAY

She tried to watch for the movement of the hands on the silent clock. It had been a game, now it was therapeutic. She had insisted on his taking the wallwagger out of the sun-lounge and putting it in the spare bedroom. The insistent thud was an annoyance. As with so many things, she no longer had the luxury of acceptance. Once, her impatience had sprung from strongly held belief, now she was often just irritable.

All morning she had fretted. The clear sea and sky would make the passage easy for the mainland boat. It was chugging out across the bay now, crawling towards them like a beetle. When it rounded the second island her husband laid aside his book.

'I'd better go down – in case.'

'You should have written, told her not to come. I asked you often enough.'

'It's not likely she'll come. She's been threatening it for years, why should she suddenly do it now? I'll just walk down for the papers. I'll get the tea when I come back. Is there anything you need before I go?'

'Nothing.'

'I'll be back in the hour.'

'Yes.'

'You're all right?'

'Yes, yes, yes, I'm fine.'

He had aged in the last six months. His handsomely weatherworn face had become haggard. The colour was going from his skin. He would be close to death himself if she didn't go soon but distance was impossible to gauge. It couldn't be too far away but she couldn't be objective. Some kind of defence went up when she thought of it. Not fear but ignorance, perhaps, or inexperience. She smiled at the thought and rubbed the persistent, gnawing spot on her stomach. She eased out Florrie's letter from the pile on the wicker table. It was not necessary to read it but she checked the post date for assurance. It had arrived six weeks earlier. Florrie wouldn't come now. It was, as he'd said, a yearly promise. She didn't want to see Florrie. They had trained together at Carysfort in the thirties. Florrie had come out each summer when first they'd moved to the island but over the years the trips had become more and more infrequent. The last time they had met had been in Ballina three summers back. But she didn't want to be seen this way, not even by Florrie, not as a misshapen, grossly pregnant old woman. If Florrie came now, she would hate her for not sensing that she was unwelcome.

Sometimes she wished she were like Florrie – not that her life hadn't been happy, tinged with the idyllic, even. But she wondered, more and more now, if the illness hadn't grown, diabolically, out of the children's births. There must be some connection back to them. As she thought about it, she found herself overcome with a desire for the gift of sin, for some of Florrie's style – impending death had brought a strange, almost orgasmic, need for profanity, irresponsibility.

Looking up from the shore, she dwelt on the ruin of a house five hundred yards from the beach, a house with three chimney stacks and the remains of properly fitted window ledges, which had, when they arrived in 'thirty-nine, seemed the essence of boldness and pride and now looked merely foolish. The Halligans had lived in the house then, returned from America with money and ideas, building this enormous place in the face of the wind and the Atlantic waves, a baronial hall on lands they had once been forced to leave in poverty, lands which, through improvidence, they had had to leave again. By the mid-fifties, when the other islanders were coming slowly to prosperity, the Halligans were in some miserable flat in Birmingham. The foolishness and stupidity of people. And to think she had once taken it for quiet philosophy!

It had been one of the Halligans who had come up to this house a week after their arrival and knocked loudly on the back door. She had opened it while Michael went on painting behind her. The man outside was carrying a split fuchsia root.

'I'm Danny Halligan. I live in the house above. I heard ye were here. I wanted to say welcome. Ye're recent wed they tell me. There's a custom in the place that the family splits a root of bush for the newlyweds to plant in their own place. Ye've none here, so bein' neighbours I brought this across.'

He proffered the bush, root first. He had spoken quickly, confidently. She invited him in.

'No, ye've work to do,' he said, peering in at Michael. 'Another time. If you're in need of anythin', drop down to me.'

The fuchsia had grown in the back garden until the mid-sixties. They had cut it down then, rotten and gnarled. Margaret had carried a spray of it in her bouquet.

She started awake, sweat running down her face and neck, the heat in the glass-panelled room was stifling. There were voices on the road. Michael talking and a woman's voice. She pushed the sweat back into her hair. Michael came in the gate. Mrs Kane went on, up the hill road.

'Were you all right?'

'Yes. I dozed off, it's hot in here. Open the window.'

'I got all the papers.'

He left the bundle on the arm of her chair. In winter the papers were often a week late. Even in summer there was always a doubt about their arrival. Today they were all there, even the English ones.

'I'll get some tea and a bit to eat – it's all ready, just to put up.'

She left the papers undisturbed. She had never been very interested in what they had to say. You heard the worst of it on the radio – the rest was irrelevant.

The children had written, earlier in the year, urging him to take her to Dublin for treatment. It had been a concerted effort – she'd have the best of doctors, he could stay with them, she'd have every chance. They hadn't gone so far as to suggest she'd live any longer, only that there would be no shortage of possibilities. But she was adamant. She was staying here. Michael had imagined it to be some kind of attachment to the place but it wasn't really, not any more. It was hopelessness. She would like to be off the island, to slip into the water in its coolness and take her time, stopping off at the small island before drifting to the mainland and some undefined torpor.

When the growth had become pronounced they had travelled to Dublin and stayed with Margaret in Blackrock. A line of two-foot-high walls dividing neat back gardens, each with its metal spinning clothesline and wooden tool shed. As empty and foolish as this place. Coming back, they had run into rain in the bay and getting out of the boat she had stumbled on a wet plank. Two of the young fellows on the boat had laughed.

'Jasus, look at the thighs on that wan,' one of them had whispered.

'Home on the range,' the other sniggered.

She had held on until she got home and then locked herself in the bathroom and sat on the toilet, weeping. She had taught those boys. All they saw in her were swells of white flesh glimpsed under a heavy skirt on a fish-smelling pier. Was anything lower?

Michael came in with plates, ham sliced thinly, lettuce, tomatoes, scallions, boiled eggs, salad cream in a neat blob on the side. Too much of everything.

She felt sick, even at the sight of it. He went back for bread and tea. He placed them quietly on the small table.

'Salt,' he muttered, going out again.

'Florrie didn't come.'

'Not at all, too comfortable. She won't come. Islands were never her forte, even in the early days this place was too quiet for her. Not enough men.'

She nibbled at a piece of lean ham.

'You look a bit better.'

She despised him for this unnecessary lie. They had talked things out rationally, almost like planning a room, when she had first found out. Now it wasn't referred to because Michael, like herself, was wary of things he couldn't date and quantify.

'Close the window, will you, it's cool.'

There was little or no wind but she was chilled at the sight of the sea, which always seemed black now and swelled instead of rippling onto the sand. When first they had come out here, it had been blue through the summer and well into the autumn. They had cycled to the outermost point of the island to watch the sun come up across an unbroken plate of azure and then hurried back to be in time for school, holding the shared sight in their separate rooms until they could struggle home, exhausted, to bed.

One Saturday, just after she got pregnant for the first time, she had gone out to the Head. Michael had been putting glass into the school cloakroom windows. She had found a sheep caught in the barbed wire. She had tried to free the animal but, in its fear, it backed onto the cliff edge. An old man had come from a field and loosed the animal.

'Always better to lave them be. They're worse if you interfere with them. Always get out in the end themselves.'

'Thanks.'

'Takes time to learn things, Mistress.'

'Call me Betty, that's my name.'

'Better to call you by your station, to my line of thinkin'.'

That had been the first time she met Paddy Lenihan.

'Do you remember Paddy Lenihan?'

'Of course. What put him into your mind?'

'I was just thinking.'

He looked at her worriedly and then thought it better to humour her. 'They were great times, starting here.'

'Yes.'

'Ideal, really.'

'A bit worn, a bit clichéd.'

He said nothing.

A special effort, she thought. I'm hurting him.

'The new pair are happy enough,' he said.

'The dream again. The sooner all the children are sent to the mainland school the better. It might get rid of this damned insularity.'

He was silent. He wouldn't be drawn. Too bloody considerate. He began clearing away the tea things, as he had done every Sunday.

In the beginning they had been alone and then Galvin, the parish priest, made a habit of dropping up for his tea on Sundays, arguing about Spender and MacNeice and Auden.

'Galvin was narrow,' she said when Michael came back from the kitchen. 'He pretended jocoseness but it was all sniping stuff. He was like the rest of this place – scratch the skin and you'll find fear. Oh, it was all good fun – "MacNeice is a Communist." He knew nothing about it. The catch cries of a clown.'

Michael stood at the table, waiting for her tirade to end. She finished and waved him away.

I wish to Christ he'd argue, fight. Seeing me out in kindness. Like his sneaking off one Friday to arrange for the grave – a badly kept secret at Christmas, she thought. She'd known where he was gone. She'd picked a site but never bought it and he had sidled off to make sure she got what she wanted.

The cemetery was hidden from the mainland. When they had first come out all they could see were three ruins. The place had a deserted look. The houses were nestled into the rock and the school and church sat in an opening of stone on the bend of the island, towards the sea but protected by the hills. The cemetery was on the ocean side, along a road that went beyond the last house and petered into a track for its last four hundred yards. She had developed a fear of that windward, seaward side of the island. It was like being put away, thrown to the ocean. Out there no one was living. She had visions of wandering isolate between the headstones of people who had been dead years before her birth, people who would have no welcome for her because they knew her real feelings. When she listened at night to the sea she was terrified at its closeness and, most of all, by the knowledge of death's presence within her.

She heard the clinking of dishes from the kitchen and mustered her remaining energy to know what would most hurt him, how she could break this awful comfort that had been the core of their lives and was, suddenly, humiliating.

VISITING DAY

The orderlies were coming along the corridor, from the wards, pushing huge metal trolleys that rolled from side to side. If you looked carefully you could see the splashes of thin gravy from the piled plates. There were occasional stains on the skirting boards of the passages and rooms where the loads had been too high and the orderlies too rushed. These were the plates from the bedridden. Their numbers remained more or less constant. As the winter came on, people who had been able to hobble to the canteen were confined to bed but there was what the attendants referred to as natural wastage and every week through the cold season a hearse would slip up the back drive and around the tactfully placed limes that separated the hospital from the mortuary chapel. And there were always new faces in the day room, people who came like infants to school and stayed on and on, waiting for nieces and nephews to take them out again, accepting the place as the weather grew warmer, searching out its good points.

Aylward hadn't wanted to come here but he had grown afraid on his own. His daughter had invited him to live with her in New England but not even the promise of spectacular autumns would draw him to America. Instead, he sold the house and furniture and got himself a room in the hospital. He had never had much money, never enough to let it talk, but with everything sold it whispered and he began to enjoy the security of the place and the reassurance of a smiling face looking around his door in the small hours.

He was fortunate. He had, he joked, as Salinger would say, his faculties intact. He could go down town, take the occasional Saturday train to Dublin and visit friends at Christmas. He would have preferred life at home but he never went near the house nowadays. He walked every road but his own. There was no point. Any branch damaged on the weeping birch, any gap in the beech hedge and he'd have come back depressed, miserable with his own fear that had made him trade little achievements for security.

He and his wife had always sailed close to the wind but that had never worried her and she had kept him afloat most of the time. It hadn't been a wonderful life but a worthwhile one.

There had been hundreds at her funeral and probably would be at his own, though when you no longer lived in an area people seemed to assume you should already be dead.

Still, he thought, he was one of the day-room dinners and his pins showed no signs of folding. He'd soldier on. So long as he maintained the knack of not looking back he'd be all right. All his life he had been dogged by worries about what he should have done and what he would have to do. That was why he had been earthed in her common sense. And then she was gone and he found himself looking to his immediate needs. There was no point in looking beyond any nightfall and he shut out the past, neatly, tightly. But today was for better things. Today was for lifting yourself up and for knowing that you only had to open the double doors and you could walk as far as any man. For knowing that if some young woman glanced at you in the street it was because she had been caught by the life in your eyes, a light that had once been strong enough to make you say outlandish things.

'Matron's on her way, people,' a tall nurse said from the doorway. The rattling trolleys, Denture Bins he'd heard them called, had been stilled in the damp bowels of the old building.

'I think we can open these doors, if you're warm enough, Mr Aylward.'

'Oh, yes, yes, of course.'

The nurse smiled.

'You look a treat.'

He believed her.

She opened the double French doors and the smell of summer came off the lawn and the trees.

'Will it last for ever?' the nurse asked, feeling the weeks of heat seeping off the orange grass.

'I hope so.'

'Me too. We're off to west Cork this weekend, for the fortnight. Knowing our luck the whole damn thing will come down in a gale for two weeks.' Then, thinking better of it, she said: 'Still, I don't suppose so. Not for your holiday. It'll be all right for that. I picked a good time, taking my holidays while you're away. You've picked the best time.'

'I think so.'

There was no doubt in his mind. It would be fine for the next ten days, as it had been for the last forty-three. You had only to look outside to know.

'Here she is now. Oh well.'

The nurse grimaced as the matron swept into the room, followed by two nurses and an orderly.

'How are we all today? In fine fettle?'

She spoke to the ceiling. A few mumbles came from the half-dozen people in the room.

'And Mr Aylward?'

He was often embarrassed by the attention she paid him when there were other patients who got more from a word than he did. But today he didn't mind.

'Very well, thank you.'

'Good, good, all set then?'

'Yes.'

'Cases all packed?'

'Oh yes.'

'That's a fine tie. Tweed. Always pays to look your best. Well, have a nice time. Do send us a postcard and we'll look forward to seeing you when you return. Sunday week, isn't that so?'

'Yes.'

'Good. All right, carry on nurse. And you will see to that window, you won't leave it open late into the evening?'

'No, matron.'

'Very good.'

She smiled from a great height. A smile that passed a foot above the heads of the inmates and then she was gone. Only the white trousers of the orderly, as he turned into the corridor, remained of the great presence.

'You got off light,' Kirwan said from the table, where he sat reading a paper.

'So I did,' the nurse laughed, 'but I'm keen at my job.'

Keen was a favourite word with Kirwan.

'Oh, y'are, I'd say y'are.'

'She gave you a great send off,' she said, turning to Aylward again. 'Must be expecting a stick of rock when you get back.'

He nodded.

'Well, I better go and see they're not beating one another with the lettuce in the kitchen. If I don't see you before you go, have a hell of a time. And let that daughter of yours spend all she likes on you, it's only once in a while. Anyway, I'm sure she will. Bye.'

'Goodbye.'

The nurse left them. Slowly he looked about the room. A woman was drowsing in the rectangle of dusty light beside the television set. Someday when it was warm, perhaps this summer, she would stop sleeping and they'd all be asked, quietly, to leave the room. At a large table two men were working on a jigsaw. Kirwan sat at the same table, reading his newspaper. He rattled it and turned a page noisily, patting down the awkward creases. Aylward turned his gaze on the garden. Two young nurses crossed the end of the lawn, on their way to the tennis courts behind the ambulance shed. He stood up and looked at the large clock over the door. Twenty past one. An early lunch and little to do. She wouldn't be here before three, not by the time she got out of Dublin. It might be much later.

He walked out to the slabbed patio that fell in gentle steps to a wide gravel path that ran about the acres of lawn. On the right were thinned woods and on the left open fields. If you walked to the end of the lawn you were in sight of the river. From which they were warned like children. Yet every year one or two of them made it that far and slipped away, down through the busy town and between the bottles and milk cartons and beer tins at the bridge where the new line crossed the water. Most of them stopped there, caught on the dam where the slow, wide, sweep turned white and poured into the narrow cleft between the island and the open country-side. Occasionally, a frail body would go over the dam and be away for days, temporarily free. And then there was Martin who had known he was dying, who had known his own weakness. He had got away from the ward one evening last October, scrabbled his way at the lock on these doors until he forced them open, leaving torn splinters the fresh paint couldn't cover, and walked or crawled the length of the lawn and through the first field. They found him early the next morning, caught on the heavy barbed wire at the bank of the river, crying every time he heard the wheep of water on the dusty reeds fifteen yards away. Last October. They'd taken him down to St Dympna's, he was still there and would be, insane in the knowledge that he had almost made it away from the pain that was doubled by survival. Aylward was lucky. He had his faculties and could choose what he remembered.

He sat on the warm, wooden seat that had replaced the extraordinarily uncomfortable wrought-iron affair presented to the hospital by the local Lion's Club. He would enjoy the hour or two of anticipation.

'The big day, hah?' Kirwan sat down beside him.

'Yes.'

'What time is she due?'

'In the afternoon.'

He did not want company now and particularly not from this man.

'Long time since she was home. Not since the missus died.'

Aylward said nothing.

'There's a thing I've noticed about you,' Kirwan said. 'The way the place seems to sit around you, like it was yours, because you have a room. You're not the only one with a room. Only a question of spondulicks, nothin' else in it, y'know. Nothin'.'

'What are you talking about? I didn't ask you to talk to me.'

'Not at all, no. Why would you? What am I? A banjaxed plumber with a bollicksed leg, hah?'

'I don't know what you're driving at, Kirwan, but I've no intention of listening to this kind of nonsense. Why don't you take it elsewhere?'

Aylward stood up quickly.

'Your missus wasn't like that. Not in the least bit stuck-up. Far from it.'

'What are you saying?'

'Nothin'. All I'm sayin' is, she was a friendly woman. Meet you with open arms.'

Aylward looked down at the black mouth of the crippled man.

'You're pathetic, Kirwan. Did you think you could hobble along here with your insinuations and ruin my day? Did you really think that? As if we weren't close enough for my wife to tell me about you. I know everything. I've known it all along. Did you imagine you were that important to her?

A dalliance. For Christ's sake, what were you? A month's mistake when we were married, something that happened before we settled down. I know everything about you and her and that isn't much. It was over bloody quick.'

Aylward was caught between the delight of his knowledge and his anger at this man's attempt to ruin everything.

'By God, you're low,' he said. 'I've never liked you but I didn't think you crawled this close to your belly.'

Kirwan's mouth was still a dark grin. Aylward turned to go back inside.

'Avvy.'

Aylward hadn't heard the name for twenty, maybe twenty-five, years. A pet name his daughter had given him.

'What did you say?'

'You heard me bloody clear, mister. Give her a few jars and she'd talk. Over bloody quick, hah?'

Aylward felt himself drain as he stood over the other man. He almost reached for Kirwan's arm as he lowered himself onto the bench.

'Did you think you could badger her like you done the childer? She knew the low, crawlin' bastard she was married to. What did you call it? A dalliance. You had a word for everything. It was safe if you knew about it, you could put a stop to anythin' you knew about.'

They sat, looking out on the lawn and the pieces of the town that stuck above the distant bushes. For all the world, two elderly men enjoying the sun.

'Why are you going on like this . . . now?' Aylward whispered. 'Why are you trying to break up the past?'

Kirwan gave a short, sarcastic laugh.

'It doesn't matter. It's no matter to her where she is and we're old enough and near enough to it ourselves to know it doesn't matter.'

Aylward felt the day slipping from him. He must do something to regain it.

'If you think you're going to take the pleasure of my holiday from me you're mistaken.'

'I'm just sittin' here, talkin', passin' time with you,' Kirwan said. His face was open now, like a child's. 'If you think I'm goin' to run up and tell her about her mother, you're worryin' for nothin'.'

'Then why are you saying all this to me?'

'I'm sayin' it. I'm sayin' it. I'm just sayin' it. Why not?'

'You're lying.'

Kirwan breathed out, loudly, and shook his head. After a long time he spoke, slowly and clearly.

'I just want you to know there's nothin' special about you or me. And there was nothin' special about her, no more nor anyone else. We're all the one. So long as you know that.'

'What you say doesn't matter to me,' Aylward said. 'We lived out our lives. She told me about you. There's nothing you can do.'

Kirwan seemed not to have heard, he seemed never to have been part of the conversation. Another nurse hurried across the lawn.

'The weather'll hold,' Kirwan said. His chin was resting on his palm and his elbow was cradled on his crossed knees. His right eye was almost closed and with his left he stared into the space of the sky.

'She kept me going,' Aylward said, with strength in his voice. 'She did it because she knew she was doing right. Not because she was apologising. You can't go on doing that all your life. You make mistakes and you get over them. You're the one who never did.'

Aylward nodded, reaffirming his pity for the other man.

'Melissa, isn't that what you called the young one? A fancy name.' Kirwan said. Then he stood up, as if to get a clearer view of the sky and what it might hold. 'Take a look at her. See if there's all of you in her.'

Aylward jumped to his feet.

'What are you insinuating?' he shouted.

'Hah, I'm not saying she's mine, don't let that get you excited. But look at her. She's a well-grown woman now. See if there's a shadow there. Bad blood will out, isn't that what you said to your missus?'

He shuffled away down the path and around the corner to the day room.

Aylward was only vaguely aware of his going. Then he became aware of the sun off the river but that held nothing for him. He thought about Martin caught on the barbed wire, crying and struggling. He felt bitterly sorry for him. He knew how he must have felt.

Melissa would want to see the house and drive up to the graveyard before they left town. But it would come to an end.

When he returned from his holiday he would ask for permission to visit Martin. He would avoid Kirwan. All of these things could be done.

For now he must wait for his daughter. Already he was afraid of who she might be.

ABSENT CHILDREN

People think because we collect shite that we are shite. They never seem to realise how much we see into their little lives. What they shite, what they drink, what they puke, what they eat. It all ends up in the bins, doesn't it? And we see them for what they really are. You are what you throw in your bin, isn't that it? Bloody sure it is. So don't come the heavy with us. We see it all, friends, and then some.

I mean, some people throw everything out, good as new. Others throw nothing out. You can see stuff building up in their garages, in their yards and gardens, flowing out through gateways but still they hang on to the last little bit.

I mean, you see it all. Like a few weeks back I was doing the early round, right in the middle of that frigging heatwave and I was not, I mean bloody not, prepared for pissing about. But still, even in a circumstance like that you try to be a little bit, you know, discerning, you try not to fuck things up completely. Not totally. I mean, you get guys working with you who do fuck things up and automatically, without really trying, it just comes as natural to them as shit to a pig. But I try not to be like that. I meet weirdos, very strange, I mean very, very strange, people but I try to take most people as I find them. Never assume, that's what I say. Never assume, never presume. Take things as you see them. Fair's fair. I mean, that is the way to tread, isn't it?

Anyway, this morning, whatever morning, we were out doing the early run and one of the blokes is a street ahead, lining up the bins for us on one side, speeds things up instead of criss-crossing all over the place. There is a method, you know, to everything. Collecting shit has its own method, believe me.

Anyway, we swing into the road and he's walking past us, on his way to the next one, and he says to me – I just saw a fuckin' lunatic woman out scrubbing the street.

What? I said.

Scrubbing the road with a brush, there, he says, pointing to a damp patch on the road outside one of the houses.

Maybe she's Islamic, I said, throwing the head towards Mecca.

Fuckin' header, he says, throwin' the head towards the nuthouse.

We walked down the road he had just come off. The damp patch was outside a house like any other but so what? I've seen people manicuring their lawns with scissors at six o'clock on frosty mornings. There's no accounting for taste.

My clever comrade had thrown a bicycle on top of the two bins outside this house, a child's bicycle. Now, sometimes it's hard to tell shite from possessions, I know, but there are places where you draw the line and a kid's bike with one handlebar bent is not our kind of thing. I threw it back onto the lawn of the house and hoisted the first bin into the feeder bay. I turned back to get the second bin and a woman came running from the door of the house.

Take it, for Christ's sake take it, she was shouting.

Take the bicycle, take it.

She was screaming.

Okay, I said, I'll take it. I thought it was there by mistake.

Take it, she said again.

But she wasn't screaming now. The words came out in short bursts of breath.

I'll take it, I said. No big deal.

I shoved the second bin up onto the feeder and then left it back on the path. I lifted the bike and hung it on the feeder bar. There was no way I was throwing a perfectly good bike into the feeder. Anyway, she didn't even notice. She had gone back up her path and was closing the front door by the time I got to the next house.

Like I say, there's no accounting for taste. If someone wants to get rid of a good TV, a good sofa, a good bike, I'm happy to oblige. I have a shed full of stuff and people come and look at it and, eventually, it all moves.

I straightened the handle on the bike. There's a bloke coming to see it this evening. He wants a good second-hand bike for his young fellow.

I have just the job, I told him.

That's the way it goes, swings and roundabouts. I mean, that's the way it goes, isn't it?

HEWER

He stood in the rectangle of shadow where the sun from the
door and window had not reached. He felt the softness of the
shavings under his feet. Felt them as he had done for years.
The workshop was quiet. The two men who had come in
that morning had gone home. Home, he knew, to change
their clothes, put on their good suits, wash themselves before they came back with the crowds after tea. He had wanted
to do the work himself but the boys had insisted and the two
men had come in at nine.

He ran his hand along the tight-grained wood as he did
when he had finished a job himself. He loved the feel of the
strong oak under his pushing fingers. No matter what
the job, it always had the feel of something masterfully
done. All the more so because of the finality of the
thing. Something so conclusive must be as near perfect as
didn't matter.

He walked about the workshop, passing in and out of the
sun that rested easily on the warm floor. He found himself
dragging his hand along the timber, losing concentration.
The work would be good. The boys knew what they were
doing when they asked Tommy and Mick to come in. They
had known her as long as he had himself. It had been as
important to them to do it properly as it would have been to
him. The timber sat perfectly, board into board. As yet there
was no lining. He was glad of that. He preferred the feel, the

smell, the rawness of timber. They would put the sawdust in
later and then the soft white material. They would staple it
neatly, ready for the morning. He had done it himself count-
less times.

When his sons suggested having the men in to make the
coffin he had argued. It was his responsibility, he said. If he
had made coffins for the town he could make one for his
own wife. But they insisted. Now he didn't mind. It was fine
work. He looked at the curved head, viewed it from the
doorway. Fine work.

When he stepped into the late sun he left the workshop
door ajar, as it was always left. The warmth was unseasonal
for March. For almost a week the skies had been clear and
the sun hot. He scuffed the ground at the wooden water
barrel. It was flaky with dryness, half-empty.

'Hewer of wood,' he said aloud.

He looked about him, afraid that he might have been
heard. The garden was empty, even of birds. He whispered
the words again. There had been a time when they set him
aflame with hatred. Sullivan, the teacher, had thrown them
at one of the boys, trying to make little of him.

'Your father is a hewer of wood, boy. Remember that.'

He had wanted to go down and beat Sullivan's head in but
she had cajoled him into doing nothing.

What are words? she'd said. Who cared what that lout
said? Let it rest.

And he had done nothing.

Years later they laughed about it. A compliment, she said.
But he still nursed the sting of the condescending remark.
He could imagine the biting, twisted lip as the words were

hurled. He could see the compliment, not in the words, but in what he was, hewer and shaper of timber, maker of worthwhile things. Even in death what he made was beautiful, solid. More solid than the words of a man in a schoolroom.

He was at the end of the garden now, among the rhubarb stools. The great leaves would spread out through the summer and dance in the pelting rain. At night you'd hear the rain beating on them. That and the creak of the firs and the roar of the trains picking up speed. Sounds of the night, winter and summer.

He turned to go back into the house. A corner of the garden shone in the very last rays. He had been digging there earlier in the week. The first turnings. There were colours beyond the rainbow thrown off the clogged earth, drowned in the darkness of the laurel hedge. The cleanly cut sides of the grass path led him back to the wicket gate and the yard. He glanced into the workshop as he passed. The fresh shavings were darkening, curling.

He lifted the old latch on the scarlet pantry door.

'Is that you, Pop?'

'Yes.'

'There's a cuppa here, if you want it.'

He went into the kitchen. Tim was standing by the table. Peter sat at the fire.

'I'll have it so.'

'Before the crowd come,' Peter said.

'Aye, they'll be up soon, I'd say. Soon as the Angelus is gone. Everything ready?'

'Yes.'

They drank their tea.

'Is the work all right? Peter asked.

'It's fine. You were right. The lads did a proud job. I shouldn't have kicked up a fuss. I just thought I'd like to do it but you were right.'

They said nothing. He was glad they didn't patronise him.

'Where's Susan?'

'She's upstairs,' Peter said. 'Putting in the rest of the flowers.'

'Her mother was good to take the children.'

They finished their tea. Tim cleared and washed the dishes.

'What time is it?'

'Just six.'

'They'll be here soon.'

'Yes.'

Susan came into the kitchen.

'I just put in the rest of the daffodils, they're lovely. If you want to go up and have a look . . . before the crowd.'

He pushed the door in and stepped onto the scrubbed boards. There seemed to be flowers everywhere. Daffodils, tulips, freesia. Two tables under the window were covered in a cloth of petals. There were arrangements on each side of the bed and along the old mantelpeice over the blocked chimney. Susan had made a flame of the place.

This was what she had wanted. Flowers, flowers, flowers, when she died. He crossed the room and touched the back of her left hand. The blue veins grizzled against the tip of his finger. He closed his fist over hers.

Walking to the window, he looked through the firs to the cathedral. He no longer felt uneasy with his back to her. He

121

had done last night. As if it was too early to turn away. But now he stayed at the window until Susan came into the room.

'Is it all right?'

'It's grand, girl, grand. The way she always wanted.'

'There aren't too many?'

'Couldn't be.'

She smiled at him.

'Only for you,' he said.

Susan crossed to the bed and touched his wife's hair.

'She looks grand.'

'Aye. But she got very old near the end. She was the same all her life until the last few weeks. Even the colour sort of went out of her hair.'

'She was beautiful.'

The heavy smell of tobacco filled the hall and the sitting room. Susan and Tim were in the pantry, drying the last of the glasses. Peter was crating the empty bottles. He could hear the gentle clink from the yard. Tommy and Mick would be gone from the workshop.

'There was a huge crowd.'

He didn't answer. He was thinking about how well loved she was.

Susan came in from the pantry.

'Are you all right?'

'Grand.'

'Can I get you something?'

'No, I'll just sit here till you're ready. Maybe we'd say a few decades before we go to bed.'

'Of course. Do you want to start now?'

'No, no, there's no hurry. I'm not a bit tired.'

They wound their way through the last prayers of the trimmings and got slowly to their feet.

'You'll have a cuppa before bed.'

'If the rest of you are having it.'

'Of course.'

He was lying in one of the single beds in the front room. Tim was asleep in the other. Peter and Susan had the side room. It was coming light. He looked at his watch. Gone six. He held his breath for a long time. This was only the second night they hadn't shared a bed. Last night and tonight. Never while she was alive, right up to the end.

He got out of bed as quietly as he could.

'Where are you going?'

'Out for a walk, just for a walk. It's bright.'

'You're all right?'

'Grand.'

'Do you want me to come?'

'No. I'm grand.'

'You're sure?'

'Yes.'

He put on his trousers and shirt and sports coat. He waited until he was out on the landing to put on his socks and shoes. It was light now and warm. Gently, he pushed in the door of their room. The two neighbours who had been there through the night remained as they sat. The room smelt of daffodils. He looked at his wife. She was blue and fragile.

Outside he could smell the summer coming. He walked across by the cathedral and out the Dublin road. He was glad to be clear of the town. When he got to Tullabraugher Protestant church he cut across the fields. About him, among the scattered mangles, sheep lay still. Bunches of daffodils gawked over the low stone wall of the churchyard. He went up the slope until he was out on the hill. The spire of the cathedral hid the house. Straps of smoke held the sky above the roofs. But it was not as he had hoped. He could not recapture the warmth of the days when they had come out here, when she was a thin, hardbreasted girl in nineteen forty. Out from the town on her half-day. Up through the trees and out of sight of the road. Those trees were gone. He closed his eyes but all he saw was the flowered room and the blue body.

Stupid, he thought, standing here in a damp field on a March morning. He wanted to be one with a memory but that wasn't possible in the house. The boys were good to him but they knew nothing of the real woman. How could they? Nor would they want to. It was a part of the past, of a passion that had nothing to do with family. It was too artificial up here. He had put too much store by it. You couldn't recapture everything at one time in one place. He had come up here expecting his ghost and hers to be waiting for him. But it wasn't like that. He should be satisfied with the peace that was in the house. But he had hoped for something beyond that. And he went on half hoping as he crossed back between the sheep and out onto the road.

As he walked he tried to recall that impertinence of her girlhood. The carnival dances. The way she was always almost eager for him to see her body. But he couldn't feel what it had been like. He could see but not feel. All he felt was the frazzled vein.

Susan was in the pantry.

'You went for a walk?'

'I did.'

'Is it warm out?'

'Yes.'

'That's good.'

'Yes.'

'The others are still asleep.'

'Do you know what?' he said eventually. 'She'd like to have been buried at night.'

'Did she tell you that?'

'No, I just know it. She was mad after carnival lights, strings of coloured bulbs.'

Susan waited for him to continue but he was silent.

'You must have had a wonderful life, when you were young.'

'I'm only realising how far it went in such a short time. You think you can always go back to things because they happened to you but they get dried up and tired. There's nothing worth looking at. And then it all sinks in and the pomp and carry-on isn't enough. The church and the prayers and all of that.'

Susan watched him, saw his sadness turn to bitterness, slowly. Like him, she was afraid.

ABSENT CHILDREN

There are times, when you come face to face with raw emotion, when you don't know what to say, so you say little or nothing. And there are other times when you're drawn into saying something that surprises you, leaves you in awe at your own daring.

It was like that with me. I was sitting in the yard of the house with the boy's mother. I knew her, knew her well. We'd met through all kinds of committees and things but we weren't on any kind of intimate level, we'd never had an intimate conversation in all our years. But I was sitting there with her, in the yard, two or three days after he'd been buried.

I was away when the accident happened, on a course, so when I got back and heard about it I called up to sympathise. I wasn't looking forward to it, I can tell you. But you have to get these things done. Anyway, we sat there, drinking tea, under a sunshade. The heat was just amazing. I had never experienced anything like it. I kept thinking about how difficult it must have been for the gravediggers with the ground so hard.

She was talking and talking about the little fellow and about how everytime she stepped out in the street she imagined there were flecks of his blood in the ruts of the tar.

And she stopped talking for a moment and then she said: 'You've no idea what it's like, have you?'

I was about to say, no, I haven't, but something stopped me.

'I think I have,' I said.

She looked at me. She hadn't expected me to say that.

I started telling her a story that I hadn't thought about for years, a story about four boys setting out one winter evening, it must have been in the end of January. Four ten-year-olds tramping out the road from Castledermot, the three miles to Mullaghcreelan Hill to sledge down the slopes in the frozen snow.

It must have been after four when we left the village. Each of us had something to slide on. A sack, two sacks, a wooden board, a car bonnet.

We were singing Christmas carols, well out of season – is anything more unseasonal than a carol in January? I asked this woman, sitting in the eighty-degree heat.

We weren't the only ones walking. There were dozens of people coming and going and no cars on the frozen, snow-locked roads between the village and the hill.

It was a blue-white evening with an almost complete moon hanging up over Ballyvass bog. Every tree in Mullaghcreelan wood was clear in its own space. I had never seen the trees so individually set before.

We traipsed up the path through the trees, following the shouts that guided us to where the procession of sledges shot down the incline and into the flattened furze bushes at the base of the hill.

The summit was a milling collection of hats, scarves, laughing figures whose faces were dark in the shadow of the moon.

We joined the queue and took our turns at screaming out into the chilled air and shooting helplessly into the frozen furze. It was worth the wait and worth the three-mile walk.

The stream of voices crying in helpless laughter went on and on and as one group disappeared home for tea another replaced it.

I don't remember exactly what I was doing when it happened, the accident. I may have been twenty yards away, on the other side of the hill, and then everything seemed to go silent and I turned and saw the adult figures disappearing awkwardly now, all their grace at sliding gone, over the edge of the hill. The children stood on the brow, staring down. I ran across to join them. A huddle of coats stood at the bottom of the slippery run, out beyond the furze, where the snow gave way to the darkness of the evergreens. Somewhere between them a figure lay on the whiteness.

'She went out over the furze,' someone whispered, as if what the figure had done was deserving of awe.

We stood there for seven, ten, minutes and then one of the men at the foot of the hill took off his heavy overcoat and draped it across the dark figure on the ground and we knew, without being told, that the girl was dead.

I remember her name. Miriam Thompson.

Another of the men came up the hill and took the car bonnet we had and brought it down and lifted the girl's body onto it. He and two other men began to carry it down through the trees.

The four of us followed, I think only because the bonnet was ours and we were determined not to lose it.

The men carried it down and hoisted it over the stepping stones onto the road.

'No cars coming in this weather,' one of them said and they set off walking for Castledermot.

We followed behind, gradually closing in on them.

At one point, coming through Hallahoise, one of them slipped and the coat slid from the girl's face. It was perfectly white in the moon and there was one slight bruise on her temple.

'That couldn't have killed her,' I said.

'She broke her neck,' one of the men said.

I didn't understand what that meant but I nodded anyway.

The longer we walked the colder it got, and the colder it got inside me. I began to shiver and I wished the men would walk faster. Coming in to Castledermot we met a group coming out. They already knew about the accident, though how I never knew. One of them was her father. Miriam Thompson's father. He took one corner of the bonnet, never lifted back the coat or anything, just took the corner, as if it had been left for him all those miles.

I was too numb to cry. I just let the procession drift away from me, ahead of me, and I turned at MacDonald's corner and walked home alone.

'You still have no idea what it's like,' the woman said.

I have, I have, I kept thinking. But I said nothing.

THE FALLEN

For Frank and Breege Taaffe –
from whose home the Hannons went
to join the fallen

I wore a lavender skirt that night, a slate and brittle blouse. There is a lavender skirt thrown across the chair. A different skirt. Outside, the dark says autumn. A thick mist trembles into drops on the lead pipes. It pip pip pips the last few feet into the gutter in the yard. I turned from this same window on that night. A night in summer. I looked at what I appeared to be. I knew exactly what I was.

The road outside was just as quiet then as it is now. But that was a different quietness. That was the stillness of a summer evening as the gardens burst into a bloom of sound. The click of forks echoed, turning out the last settle of the deepest frost. A neighbour, borrowing, shouted, her voice rebounding from wall to wall along the gardens. Carts rasped in the alleyways as drivers backed and worked the loads of dung between the creaky gates. Girls with arms of precious roses hurried from place to secret place. The heels of love began to sound again. The heels of love were mine.

Here. I am here. Over here on the angle of the cobbled paths. Behind me the trains thunder. I despise the angle but I welcome the grass that is thick and long, cut once, perhaps, in

eight or twelve seasons. I welcome that softness and the softness of her footsteps, unheard now by those she passes in the
street. Her resolute body unseen. Her faint laughter reaching
only me and my words are caught only by her. And, perhaps, by the other old soldiers grown tired in their graves.
Men who still remember little things. Obscurities. The shining promise of a blade. The glisten of skin, caught, at last,
after all the talk. The button blaze. The lightning smile.

Did we pay too much for the pleasures we got? The things
that mattered then seem of no consequence any more.

What you want is my story.

My name is Mary Lloyd. I was born near Castledermot in
the County Kildare on the seventeenth of June, 1890. I was
the youngest daughter of three. My father was a farm labourer
who could turn a pair of horses with a twist of his wrist and
a cluck of his tongue. He cut and kept the ditches, weaving
alder, sally, elder into fences every spring. He carted grain to
Hannon's mill. He ploughed the acres pair by pair. We rarely
saw him in the summertime, except in passing, when he'd
lift us on the chestnut backs and trot us to the road. My mother
was a seamstress. Her customers left their cloth in a shop in
the town and we collected it after school, carrying the bun-
dles carefully, up and down Fraughan Hill.

By the time I was ready for work my sisters were married
and gone. I travelled twelve miles to find something new.
From the side of Fraughan, through Castledermot on a fair
day. The cattle milled on Hamilton Road, dropping their thick
necks to drink from the Lerr. Farmers and jobbers and huxters
pushed and jostled on the Square. They glanced at me. I

waited hopefully, for some remark, a whistle or a gesture. They were too busy with their money. I walked through Hallahoise, past the woods at Mullaghcreelan, by the gates to FitzGeralds' castle, on through Kilkea, Grangenolvin, to work in a bakery in Athy. I was sixteen then.

I did my work in bakery and shop. I danced. I sang. I walked with other girls on summer nights. Out past the pond at Bray and back the Castledermot road. Board dances and house dances marked the seasons of my life. I would dream men's tongues along my breasts, their lips about my nipples. I had my share of men. They had their share of me. I was twenty.

I'd see him in the street. Him and his wife. She was young. Almost as young as me. And hard. I could hear it in her voice when she spoke in the shop. They moved from Barrack Street to a cottage on the Dublin road, across from where I had my digs. I'd see him in his garden among the daffodils and dahlias. Everything in that garden had its place. The rows and lines reminded me of my father's garden, of his fields all ploughed and set. There were apples and cherries where the drunken bees hummed and fell. But it wasn't just a garden of lines. There were clumped and clustered flowers where you least expected them. They took you by surprise. And all the plants and slips in pots along the gravel near the door. All waiting to be sown or given out to people in the town.

I wonder where a passion like mine starts. How does it grow? Does it run in the blood or does it just get out of hand till it's beyond control? Is it like sap rising? Is it something that insists on being heard? I know it stares. It stares till the stare is returned. It flames until it burns its root and then it goes on burning. It outlasts time and place. I know all this because this passion for him carried me beyond any love I had accepted in the past.

I'd walk the roads I knew they'd be walking. I'd stay at home, miss dances with the other girls if I half thought he'd be there burning twigs or leaves in late October. I'd talk to his wife for ages in the hope that he'd arrive. I'd stand at the gate and stare across at him. I knew how foolish I must look but I didn't care. I was twenty-two.

I'm Frank Kinsella. I was born in this town on the seventh of October, 1880. I was an only son. My father was dead by the time I was born. He was never talked about and I never saw any reason to enquire.

I left school at twelve and started work for the Lord Kildare. The FitzGerald of Kildare. I set my mind to like the work. I walked the six miles out and back. I did my work. I was never late and I never missed a day. I listened well to every word that I was told. I watched what the other gardeners did and I knew his garden backwards by the time I was sixteen. I knew every strain of apple; every pear along the castle wall; every breed of rose; every vine in the greenhouses. Azaleas, magnolias, hydrangea. The cypresses, the oak, the ash, the elder and the clematis. There were winter mornings at Nicholastown when the frost was as thick as cream. There were evenings when the rain was like bamboo rods across my back on the straight beyond Grangenolvin.

I'd salute Lady Nesta on the driveway. I'd stop to talk to Lady Mabel on her horse. I remember Lord Walter framed in the stable doorway with a light behind him like a golden blanket, soft and clean. It was Christmas time.

It was Christmas, too, when I met my wife. At a dance in the town hall in Athy. There she was in a crowd of girls. Her face was young and clear. It was like the light in the stable yard. And her hair was wild and brambled. She had a smile as bold as brass. We were married the following autumn. New suit, a ten-pound note and two days off. Lord Walter promised to put in a word about a cottage on the Dublin road. He was as good as his word.

She was hard at times but so was I. I could swing a fist with the best of men on Barrack Street. But she could soften too.

If you asked me to name a time I'd go back to a summer morning. It was four or five o'clock. We'd been to a dance somewhere near Baltinglass and we were freewheeling down from Mullaghcreelan. The light was just coming up and it was a warm morning. Sometime in the end of June. We weren't even tired after all the dancing and a ten-mile cycle. We were laughing as we reached the bridge above the Griese. We stopped and I lifted her onto the parapet above the river. I climbed down to pick a water iris from the bank. The river was down to a trickle and the bank was cracked and baked. I remember my boots made an impression on the mud. I looked up. She was perched above me. And then a man rode past, dismounted, pushed open a gate into a field and wheeled his bicycle across the grass. He had a small white box tied to the carrier. We watched until he disappeared into the ruins of a church. I climbed back up and handed her the irises. She dropped them slowly in the water and we watched them sail between the rocks and out of sight. Oh, she could soften too.

She never loved me the way I was in love with her but I accepted that. I saw this as how our lives were going to be. The same as everyone I knew. She could be soft but the softness disappeared and she had a habit of denying the memories I had. I'd remind her of things and she'd pretend to remember nothing. She'd be angry if I went on about it. I never understood how she could swear the past away. And once she started that, I knew I loved her as little as she loved me. I'd think to myself that she could change as much as she liked and so would I. But she should leave the past alone.

At times she'd say she was bored. Another time it was loneliness. 'You have the garden,' she'd say. 'The garden doesn't mean the same to me.'

One of her brothers would cycle in in the mornings and they'd cycle out together. After work I'd call to her father's house and collect her. Winter and summer she'd be there, curled up like a cat beside the fire. Once or twice, when it was raining, she said she'd stay. Then more and more I'd hear that story. 'You go on,' she'd say. 'There's no sense the two of us getting wet. I'll stay the night.'

Never once was I asked to stay. She never suggested it and her father and brothers made no move. I knew they'd never have me sleeping under their roof. As far as they were concerned, she was still one of them. I'd go home and walk around the garden. I remember one wet spring evening in particular. I walked around and around the cottage, up and down every path. There was a fine rain falling and there was a yellow light from the sun over the Laois hills. Around and around I walked. Other times I'd check the potato pits or heel in cabbage plants. I'd smoke a pipe. Some nights I'd sleep there in the chair. I'd wake at two or three and toss another sod on the melted flames. In the end the winter won. The blankets burnt with a better heat. I could imagine then.

She came some Saturdays. I'd arrive and find her there. The house would smell of bread and her. The hearth would be swept. I always kept it swept but this was in a different way. More complete. The windows would be open and the washing done, flying a flag of possibilities. She'd stay till Monday. I'd begin to tell myself the past was past. And then I'd find her gone again. I'd say nothing and neither would she.

Sometimes, I think, she was on the edge of touching me. I don't mean touch. I don't mean tease or sting. She was on the edge of explaining what was there or what was missing. Or so I thought. I never could be sure.

One Wednesday, the end of April, I drove a cart into the town to collect some seed from the railway station. I saw her father and her brothers at our gate. They had her dresses and her coats across their bicycles. One of them was coming down the path, his arms spread out. He had a mirror and a picture in them. They knew I saw them and they stood like frozen cattle, watching me. I jigged the horse and carried on.

She came to see me once after that. One evening of that week. We talked about nothing. She walked the garden with me. She was full of chat about the flowers and the plants. She'd touch my sleeve. She'd sweep the hair back from her face and stare at me, a thing she hadn't done for months. She was a girl full of courting tricks again, except I knew she wasn't. There was nothing to it. She was safe. Her bits and bobs were gone by then. She was as safe this last time as if it had been her first. And then they came to bring her home.

I'd meet her on a Sunday, safe between her brothers, on the steps after Mass. The way they carried on you'd think I was something to be afraid of. As if by then I even cared.

The whole town knew. I'd hear it in the bakery and in the shop. Every tongue had a different twist. It was because of this or that. Because he wouldn't touch her. Because he never stopped. There were always two sides at least, and every side was talked about and twisted. It wasn't that she was telling anyone. She'd still come into town but she talked as much to me as anyone and there was never a word about him or them. And he never talked. I never saw him talk to anyone. But that didn't stop the hints. By May the whole town knew.

What could I do? I was caught. Marooned. Too soon to try to make a bridge but the gap cried out for me to fill it.

Through May his garden stayed untouched, and then one evening after rain I saw him, scythe in hand, the nettles crashing from the ditch. The drops reared up and shone in every light. His sockets were still and his arms moved in them, floating rather than flapping. His head was half bent. His body was as hard as granite. I leaned across our gate and stared at him. Every now and then the blade would catch the stony wall and rasp and spark. Then it swished the wet and stinging greenery. I could hear the clean, flailing sound as clear as water. He was silent in his work, each swing was measured as he worked along the garden, never going back, the nettles laid as neat as corn across the grass.

I loved him then, by Christ I loved him then.

137

I wanted those arms to disentangle themselves from the work of scythes, from whatever memories of pleasure or pain that kept them straight. And I didn't care what it was that had driven them apart. Too much pain. Too much demand. I could coax or satisfy. Listen, I wanted to shout, I'm not afraid of what the people think or what the people say. I've watched until I know the flex of every sinew in those arms. I know the stoop, the stretch, the walk, the watch.

My name is Mary Lloyd. I start my day at six. I try to meet you or to see you as I leave for work. I rarely do. I carry bread from bakery to shop. I think about you. I think, she's the one that left but it's me that you ignore. I've seen you talking to her, hung there between her brothers after Mass.

Frank Kinsella, my name is Mary. Mary Lloyd.

I'd drive the four-pronged fork into the bitter earth. I'd push the tines a foot below the soil. I'd stoop, as I had stooped all day, and then I'd lift and free the prisoner of a winter I'd allowed to drag itself into the summertime. I'd speed the rhythm gradually. I'd thrust, then push, then stoop, then lift. And thrust and push and stoop and lift. And thrust, push, stoop, lift. Thrust, push, stoop, lift. I dug my way out of the past. I dug myself a shallow grave from which to breathe, in which to rest. I thrust and push and stoop and lift and then I hear this voice that frightens me because it seems to come from nowhere.

'My name is Mary Lloyd.'

'I know your name.'

'Tomorrow is my birthday. I'll be twenty-three.'

I smile, I can think of nothing to say and so I smile.

'I'd like it if you'd walk with me. If you have nothing else to do.'

I smile again. I say, 'Of course.' I have no idea why.

My name is Mary Lloyd, I say, as I walk back from work. I hurry now along the cobbled street. I am anxious to be out of these working clothes. I brush the flights of flour from my hair as I walk. I smile at people. I want to stop and tell them about the possibilities and still I do not want to stop. I want to hurry. I nod and rush on past the Railway Bar, across the bridge, out by the manse and through the yard into the house. I prepare myself. I wear a lavender skirt. My blouse is a slate and brittle grey.

We walk across the town. I don't care who looks or what they say or what it means. Neither, I'm sure, does he. I talk. It is uneasy talk but I go on talking and he laughs. Sometimes he smiles but his smile is as uneasy as my talk. Mostly he laughs. I can recall every moment of that walk.

We go on walking several nights a week. On Sundays we cycle out between high ditches. He calls for me. Comes and stands at the gate. Leaning across his bicycle, he talks to the woman of the house. He says goodnight at that gate. And sometimes, when I am early, I stand at his gate. Once he invites me in to smell the roses by the wall.

The summer passes. What do I notice? Fifty factory girls are burnt alive in England. I read about them in the newspaper. They are not me. I notice his garden. I notice how his face will cloud and clear. I notice her whenever she's about. She smiles at me in the shop.

I travel home one Saturday to see my sister's child. I travel back on Sunday afternoon. I ride in a sidecar to Kilkea and walk the rest of the way to be in time to meet him after tea. That evening we walk out past Lord's Island. We walk beyond the horse bridge, across the fields along the Carlow road. We perch on a half-built cock of hay and gradually slide until our backs are resting on the scattered wisps. He talks and talks instead of touching me.

That night I notice the dahlias touched with rust inside his gate. Lying awake, his plant of stock outside my window, I think how I would relish sin. But he has been so rigid in his hard red boots. His collar starched and done. I wish that I could dance the seven veils. I think about how he went on talking while the possibilities narrowed and shrank with the light.

Walking back along the railway line, he'd told me. I remembered word for word.

'She never loved me the way I was in love with her but I accepted that was how our lives were going to be.'

I waited for the rest. I waited for the recognition that I knew he had to have. If he couldn't put the words in place, if he couldn't give, at least he had to recognise what I was telling him with every gesture. I waited for him to say she had never loved him the way he knew I did. I lay and smelt the stock in the blue-black night. I imagined his tongue on mine, his fingers travelling between my thighs, his lips collapsing on my skin. In the end I knew there was a depth of pleasure and I knew as well that he'd never say that kind of thing. Not this side of whatever grave he'd already dug. Was that to be our only bed?

I envied her her passion.

If she'd talked of it. If she had put some shape on it. If she had turned to touch. I talked and talked in the hope that she'd grow tired of my talk and despairing of ever kissing me, kiss me then.

I envied her her passion.

If she had skirted it. If there had been a breath. I strained and strained to say something. To move. To step out of that grave. I tried at night to put the whole thing into words. I wanted to unhook the lust from its silent pier. But then, I thought, I know nothing about that sea. What am I? A silent inland walker, scrabbling for some other words to say the words for me.

One morning I went and sat on the low wall at the road. I measured the steps that would take me to her window. I counted the possibilities. I decided on bringing her to my house. I rehearsed the possibilities. I went back inside and lay down and felt her touch in my own. I felt the possibilities seep away.

But I envied her her passion.

I thought the smell of stock must smother her in what I felt for her. Did it not tell you everything, Mary? Mary Lloyd.

I envied him his strength.

Never mind the strength to work all day and then to work on through the night. I envied him his strength to take whatever came. To let her go when she decided she was gone. And I envied him not taking what was there of me. He could have done at any time. He need never have asked. I envied him that. In spite of everything, he must have known that I was his. I envied him his strength and damned him into hell for it.

I looked at him and saw a blind and stumbling plough horse. I thought of how my father turned his horses with a twist but I couldn't turn him any way. He was too heavy to ignore. Too set to change his ways. His boots were like brown lead feathers. His eyes were set on the end of some long drills that stretched like graves and graves and graves.

I envied him his strength, but Christ, I wished that he could sense the lust, the passion trapped in every breath I drew. Could he not feel it in my fingers; hear it in my darkest gasp; smell the smell of love that frightened me with its strength? Could he not untie the harness and touch me, just this once? Could he not take some lessons from the songs he hummed or from the thoughts his body sowed in me?

I waited.

We talked about the earliest dead who had fallen in France. They were not me.

After the harvest, after apple picking, he kissed me and I eased his hands about my body. He talked about breaking from the pier. I didn't understand but urged his fingers on. He was changing, becoming another man. I thought about the curves of his body and the curves of mine. I thought of this in the early frost, hurrying to work. I thought of it in the warmth of the shop. I gave myself to it. I drew his tongue between my lips and refused to let him go. When his touch was not enough, I touched with him. I no longer cared about the smile his wife carried. I smiled myself.

Sometimes we talked about the names we'd heard. About the dead swept back on a tide of blood at Mons. About floundering sailors from the *Cresy* and the *Hogue*, sucked into the icy sea. I felt the blood pumping like water in a millrace. I felt his mouth suck my breasts between his lips. My blood drove towards one moment, all day it drove towards the moment of release.

And then he told me he was going. I asked him why. It seemed too simple to ask that question but I had the right to ask him why. I had nothing else to say. He just smiled. A wry smile. A mirror of his smiling wife? I knew then that when we'd touched we'd hardly touched at all.

Mons, Ypres, Paris. What had these to do with me?

Nothing. And nothing to do with me. They were places where things were clear. In a minute of foolishness I had told her part of what I thought. If I went, there was some chance the past would change here the way it was changing everywhere else. I had this vision of coming back and finding my wife gone, dead, something unforeseen. Something would happen that could never happen while I was here. I believed that. She looked at me when I said that. There was something of that other, brassy look. There was no anger. Just sadness.

Nothing will change unless you change. We could go and live in another place. There's nothing here that I can't live without. I'd be happy out of here. And I have no need of rings or churches or words. None. I could gladly go without them all. You've never changed. Your wife won't be gone. She won't be dead. But there are other things that could die. Will die. Things are changed already. Why? I have the right to ask you why.

For once I thought that touch instead of words would stop the questioning. We were under the chestnut. It was raining. If I was to tell her why, what would I say? I had no idea why. It might be to escape. Or to evict. My fingers moved with ease, my tongue was sure. The rain dripped in a great circle from the widest branches while we lay in their umbrella. There was no escape. Her breath quickened and then became a question. Why?

There were other mouths that called me traitor from the corners of the street, from black doorways, from the market crowds. I never raised a fist. I ignored the mouths I could have bruised or broken easily. But I felt no satisfaction knowing how they longed for pain and were denied it by my fists hanging limp. If there was a betrayal, it had happened a long time ago.

I had no interest in the tunic or the buttons or the guns. They were part of a cause. I wasn't going for a cause. I wasn't going out of reason but out of hope.

What did I hope? That if I went I'd come back a different man. If nothing had changed, at least I would have changed. And coming back, I'd find the same woman.

But did I believe? I believed that she'd remain. But her question dimmed and quenched the hope.

Do you believe in everything you've said?

I believe you will remain.

What else do you believe?

I'll tell you now. I've said it often enough to myself. I'll tell you now. I believe in the beauty of your breasts, in the form of your shoulders, in the sickle of your thigh, in the ease of your hands, in the power of your eyes, in the fury of your hair, in the storm of your whisper, in the passion of your thought.

Do you believe in everything you've said?

No. I don't believe in me. My past is a nightmare. I have never told you that. First there is penance. Then sleep. Then this dream.

Is that the truth?

Part of the truth. The truth has nothing to do with us. The truth has all to do with me. Everything we have done has been true. The places have always been true for me – fields, gaps in ditches, trees that were one way in winter and one way in spring. Ways that you lay or laughed or walked. Ways I prepared for meeting you. These have all been true. There's no question about these. But I have no answer about why. No answer for myself, much less for you.

When you smile your mouth reminds me of your wife's.

That might be what you see but that has nothing to do with the truth.

I saw no hope.

I told no one until the thing was settled but already they knew. I gave my notice. Lord Walter asked me to think again. He said there were people he knew and then he said the job would keep.

I put straw on the pits. I got my uniform. I tied the last of the dahlias. Collected my wages. Cycled down the castle avenue without looking right or left. At home I washed in the starry yard, put on my uniform and called for her. I walked to her door and knocked. The stock was still in flower. They asked me in and ignored the uniform. We walked across the town and back. Sat on the low wall until Sunday came.

The night before he left we danced at the town hall. Sneering, I said, 'Why don't you wear your uniform tonight?' For once I saw the pain and it frightened me. I drew back from saying any more, afraid I might have said too much.
What did we do? We danced every dance while the music was playing. The music of fiddle, melodeon, piano and drum. We swung with the crowd without hearing the music. I was stunned by the speed with which certainty had arrived. Danced to the waltzes when the waltzes were playing, nodding at faces that passed in the crowd. There was Robert MacWilliams and Christopher Power, faces that passed as we swung around. He kept his distance but this moment of passion lasted as long as the music was playing. And then

146

the music stopped. The faces grew voices, the movement was over and bodies jostled towards the cloakrooms. We were part of the crowd again. Faces smiled. Mouths dribbled short ashy cigarettes. I handed in my ticket, took my coat and put it on before we walked down the stairs. Stepping out into the night, I felt neither cold nor warmth. Loud men shouted in Emily Square, peeling their bicycles from the layers against the wall. Girls laughed and waited, uncertain whether to go or stay.

We walked up Offaly Street towards the park. The cold, hard park with its shiny brown bark and its thinly frosted grass.

'Would you not bring me home this once?' I said.

'What did you say?'

'Would you not bring me home? This once.'

I brought you . . . home.

Instead of passion there was panic. He saw how easy the whole thing could have been. How simple. But he dared not recognise it. Too late for that. And I dared not say anything. Isn't that the way it was that night? Whatever our bodies did, no matter how easily, could have been done much better a thousand times after that. And whatever it was that they failed to do could be changed if there was time and ease. They did their work. The sweat of terror made the bodies slide together. It might have smelt of ecstasy but we were terrified. Our bodies ground on because it meant we had nothing to say and less time to think. And he was thinking, as I was, how this might have happened before and how easily it could have been another day on which we'd rise and go to work and come back home and go to bed. Had I not said all that? The truth was evident but there was no place for it now. I stayed and watched him dress. Had this been some kind of sweet, pale honeymoon?

We walked to the station. Him in his uniform. Me in my dancing dress. There were others there in their regalia. Their wives and sweethearts dressed for the day.

Mick Lawlor. William Wall.

I kissed him then. There on the top platform outside the stationmaster's house. We leaned against the iron footbridge and kissed. He saw, again, how easy life can be. His body hard between my twisted skirts. Until the train began to move.

Outside the station, in the silence after he had gone, I heard somebody whistle, a young shop boy on his bicycle. A song the band had played the night before: 'Night and the stars are gleaming, tender and true, Dearest my heart is dreaming, dreaming of you.' The walls closed in. I saw the throng. I smelt his sweat and I heard the music clearer than when it played. Every sense I'd stifled came alive. His smell, his touch, his taste, flowed from every pore and left me sick.

I woke up. It was another day. I had to work. I realised he had gone. I dressed and walked to the shop. Where was he now? Still in Dublin? Halfway across the sea? Somewhere in England? Certainly no further than that. I expected him to come lumbering into the shop, embarrassed, saying he had talked with Lord Walter and things had been worked out.

He was going back to gardening. He was looking for a cottage in Kilkea. It might take time but then we'd move.

I was in the bakery when one of the girls called to me. There was a man in the shop wanting to talk to me. I recognise him. Noel Lambe. He says Frank has left a key with him. He'll be keeping an eye on the cottage – sleeping there now and again. He's to give me anything I want. I'm to go there any time I want. I can stay there if I like. That's what he's been told to tell me. I have only to let him know. Any time. All as matter of fact as that.

I carry bread from bakery to shop. I chat. I clean the windows in the street.

I wake up. It's another day. I have to work. I wait and wait.

Little things that never bothered me before begin to bother me now. The weight of these boots. The way the collar scuffs my neck. The task of writing and what to say and how to say it.

'We have arrived here safely and we are training. It's not as bad as you might think. I suppose Noel told you what I said about the house. Whatever is there that you might want is yours to take.'

I don't mention moving in. I try to come to that from several ways but I can't.

I sit out in the barrack yard and try to think of other things to write. I look at the nail of moon caught on the edge of a hawthorn bush. Beyond it the lake water is dark. Darker than the Griese. But the thorn reminds me of a turn on the castle avenue. This is England. That was home. I start thinking of fields. I think of how she nested in the hollows of my body.

I think of how I wound my arms around her and nested in the hollows of her body. Her breast was in the hollow of my hand. There was a particular smell from her hair. Maybe of apples or rain. I started to say that to her and then some people passed and we went back to our bicycles and she tossed my hair with her fingers.

I don't mention any of this in my letter. This has happened. She knows that. Why write it? I tell her the food is good and the lads here are a decent crowd.

I wake and it's another day. I walk to work. I stop at his gate and notice that Noel has scuffled all the weeds. They lie in neat piles along the edge of grass. Today he will come and burn them.

I wake. This is not another day.

We cross the English Channel. It's not as bad as people say. They tell us Ypres was the worst but they tell us too that English, Irish, Germans, sang together at Christmas time. I write and tell her this.

'A happy, happy New Year.'

I am surprised at what I've written. I leave it so.

I wake and it is spring. The snow melts into isolated spots of snowdrop. The crocuses in purple-yellow dot the ground around the apple bark. And then it snows again in wintry narcissi. The evenings lengthen, carts of dung arrive from the countryside and back between the creaking hinges of town gates. Young girls I last saw as children walk with boys, out the Dublin road to Ardscull and back.

And then it is summer. I tend his garden in the evenings. Noel comes and cuts the grass. The roses rear above the walls, sweet pea rambles across the gable. I wash and clean the floors. I open drawers and find his shirts in neat lines. They smell of winter. I hang them on the line and it gives me pleasure to see them threshing in the warm wind. I leave them out overnight and tell myself as I walk to work that he is home. I almost see the smoke from his chimney. That evening I fold the shirts and put them back inside their drawers.

Noel comes and limes the walls. We sit in the kitchen talking. The sun seems caught on the hills of Laois, unable to sink. It throws a long bolster of light across the table. I ask Noel if he knows why he went. 'If you don't know, no one does,' he says. His words give me some feeling of closeness to Frank. I know what he says is true. If I don't know, he doesn't know himself. And it doesn't matter, anyway. All that matters is that next summer the three of us will sit here and then the pair of us.

His letters come. I write to him. I read his words.

We heard a story down the line today about two blokes who were sentenced for desertion. They were strapped to the wheels of a gun and shot. I don't write about that kind of thing. We hear these stories, we talk about them, but I don't write of that. I write and say things are going well. I say the weather is improving. I am glad to hear the garden is doing well and glad about the lime. The cottage needed that. I mention people I know, fellows I've met – Larry Kelly and Stephen Mealy.

In April we were at Ypres. The gas crept like stink from a tomb. We passed these men lying in the grass. Their eyes were bandaged. We could hear their screams long after we had lost sight of them. Somebody said, you can't fight that bastard gas. I didn't write of that.

I remember the autumn by its fruit. I picked the low apples. Noel climbed for the high. I came home one afternoon and found a basket left at my digs, a basket of pears sent from the castle. I walked with the other girls on October Sundays. To Bert Bridge, to the Moat of Ardscull.

At Christmas I went home to Fraughan Hill. The house smelt of damp timber and the fire shot sparks across the stone floor. I told my mother about Frank. She smiled and said nothing. On the morning I left she said, 'You'll be all right.'

We had an Easter of daffodils. They trembled and shivered. I picked some and put them in a vase on his table. I left them there, even when the petals nodded, frizzled, stumbled and fell. I left them for a very long time.

There were other things I didn't write about. I met this chap with his fingers cut so deep that they hardly seemed to be a part of him. I asked him how this happened: stretcher bearing. No stretchers left. He and the others carried the wounded on sheets of corrugated iron. He lost the use of his hands but he went on carrying with stretcher sacks tied around his neck. He told me he had carried a man two miles to the medic. Already there were thirty or forty bodies surrounding the trestle table where he worked. Still men, men screaming. The medic worked on, his vest blood-soaked. The bodies came and went, the dead and the dying. The rest were shipped further back.

The funerals begin. In the afternoon the shop shutters bang. Small cards with scrawled words appear all over the town, on doors in Barrack Street, in Leinster Street, around the Square.

I break the last branch of bloom from his lilac tree and take it home. The scent fills my room for three nights and then the bells fall apart.

One afternoon while we were marching, very close to the front, we saw a horse galloping towards us. His innards were trailing like a second tail. Then these men appeared. They came in twos and threes, the walking wounded. They came without rifles, many of them shirtless. They reminded me of people I had seen at grave sides, people deep in shock. They ignored us and went on walking, sometimes linking like drunken men on the Barrow Bridge, stupefied beyond recognition. Further along the track I saw a piece of flesh. I recognised it. Torn from the horse's belly. We went on marching.

Later, lying in a trench, waiting for the whistle, I thought about all this and then I thought of her. I knew then I would write and tell her everything – but first about the horse, the wounded, the raving mad.

His laburnum flowers fall, their golden rain scattering the grass. I get more letters from him now, full of the things he sees, the things he smells, the sounds of shells and guns and human voices. He tells me everything.

'My darling, Last week, Sunday I think, we came upon this village. It's hard to believe but it's still in one piece. It was raining when we marched in, far back from the lines. A bit like Ballitore on a wet evening. No one about. Four of us went to this little café place and sat there drinking wine. We stayed there while it got dark. You get used to wine. It's nothing like the pint of stout in Maher's but better than a lot of things I've drunk out here.

'There was this woman behind the counter. She sat there the whole afternoon and evening. She was sewing. When it got dark she lit a lamp and I could have sworn she was you. I know what you're thinking, so much for all this wine, but I swear, with the light and the colour of her hair, it could have been you. I was just sitting there watching her, and thinking to myself that I've forgotten a lot about you. About the way you look.

'The clearest memories I have are of the parts of you I saw the least. Your face only came back to me in her face and hair in the light of the lamp. You must get a photograph taken and send it to me. Then I can remember all of you. Like I say, there's parts of you I have no trouble remembering at all.

'I know what you're saying to yourself – this fellow is getting very forward.

'I've been thinking, too, about the things I'm looking forward to going back to. I made a list of them the other day. November mornings cycling out to Kilkea was the first. And then the blossoms in the castle yard. And summer evenings coming in the road when the cuckoo is raising a row in the fields. These are going to be the same as they always were. I've noticed that. No matter what changes for me over the years, no matter what sort of time I'm going through, these things always keep their magic for me.

'There's other things that will never be the same. And the things between us, they'll never be the same, only better.'

I went down to Carlow to have that picture taken. It was a Wednesday afternoon, a half-day in Athy. I took my bicycle and went alone. I was put standing in front of a tree painted on canvas.

I spent one night in a shell hole, out in no-man's-land. The artillery went on firing, the thunder never stopped. I lay there with my companion, a dead machine gunner.

When I got the photograph I put it in an envelope and sent it off to him with a letter I had written but would never dare to read.

'My dearest Frank, I've had the photograph taken and I enclose it here. I cycled to Carlow to have it done. The man there was very nice. He said all the girls are having it done. I went down on my birthday. Imagine, I am twenty-six. The photograph came on the train this evening and I collected it on my way home. I shouldn't say this, but I like it. I hope you do too. Is this the way you remember me or the part of me you've forgotten?

'It's terrible to hear what you have told me about the war. Everything is quiet here now. Sometimes I think the worse the things you write about the better it is. I feel nothing will happen to you while these things are in your letters.

'Every week now some house in the town has a black ribbon on the door and the telegram boy from the post office is dreaded when he appears in any street.

'After I read your letter, your last letter, I laid it out on the bed in your room and took off all my clothes and stood in front of your mirror and looked at myself. I was thinking of how little we've seen of one another's bodies and thinking about what you said about being different. I think you're right. But I was thinking, too, that the braver and bolder you get in your letters, the harder it is for me to be any way bold in mine. And to think I was the one was always wishing you'd do those things to me when we were out walking the Carlow road. Now I can only wish you were here to touch and kiss me the way I know you're thinking when you write your letters. You have so little time and I have all the time in the world. Don't worry, I was on my own in the house when I did that.

'I wait every day for your letters. I keep them all. I think, sometimes, you must be out of the war, the way you write such long and lovely letters. Everything here is waiting for you. Noel has the garden in fine order. The house is shining inside and out. I've painted the gate bright red. I hope you won't mind that. Everything is ready – the house, the garden, me, my body. Everything is waiting for you.

'I love you.'

I heard of a stretcher bearer who went out seven times yesterday. Each time he brought back a wounded man. The eighth time he was killed.

'My darling, I was thinking today about all the flowers I've put in that cracked jug on your kitchen table since you went away. Crocuses and snowdrops; lilacs and dog daisies and cornflowers and roses; water irises and wallflowers and dahlias now. I've picked them everywhere. Out the Barrow line, at Mullaghcreelan and Ardscull. In your garden and along the roadside out past Bray. I even brought a spray of fuchsia from Fraughan Hill.

'I wonder what flowers will be in it when you come home. Whenever it is, even in the depth of winter, I'll have flowers in it for you.'

We push to a new front line. For a time there's relief. Something new promises, but then this line, these trenches, become the same as all the others. We have been in them before or someone else has. Our lines weave. Here we are at the front line, a mile away some other uniforms are moving cautiously.

There are always stories here. New stories come with every telegram. With every corpse a story comes. One week there are four men from Barrack Street, four doors with black ribbons, eight windows with the curtains tightly drawn. Schoolchildren walk from the other end of the town to gawk. They have never seen so much death before.

I begin to fear for something. It seems there is nothing to stop this rush of dying, nothing to say the next black ribbon won't be fastened to his door. I have to get away. I leave early and travel with Noel, on his cart, to Castledermot. I walk from there. I stop to throw a penny into the Lerr at Hamilton Bridge. I wish for luck and life. For him.

Near the top of Crop Hill I meet my father taking a horse down to the forge. I walk with him. A shire horse. Brandy.

'This is the heaviest horse we've ever had,' he says. 'And he's as quiet as a lamb. Do you remember Bess when you were small? I used to put you on her back.'

I remember. Black, brown, grey and bay with a star on her forehead. 'She'd be nothing to this fellow,' my father says. 'Skin and bone.' The huge feather-feet fall as lightly as a bird's. The horse steps daintily until we reach the open forge. I stand and wait. I rename the bits of harness that my father taught us all: the cheekpiece, the blinker, the browband, the peak, the haims, the pad, the loin strap, the crupper strap, the quarter strap, the breeching strap, the bellyband, the girth, the trace bar, the rein, the bit, the noseband. I have remembered every one. I repeat them to my father and he and the blacksmith clap. The horse turns and shifts uneasily.

Walking back, my father questions me as he did when we were children.

'Would you give a horse a long drink, now, after a hot day's work?'

'No.'

'And which comes first, the food or drink?'

'The drink.'

He laughs. 'You remember well, I taught you well. I doubt your sisters would remember the half of it.' And without pausing he says: 'What about this chap of yours?'

I tell him almost everything, but not the important things.

'You'll find it hard, the two of youse, when he comes back. Things like that are all very well until they look like being permanent. Can you deal with that? The sneers and the priest

coming twenty times to your door? That'll be the easiest part.
Have you the stomach for all that? Has he?'

'We have now,' I say. 'He mightn't have had a while ago,
but we both have now.'

'Well,' my father says, 'if you're bent on staying with him
and if the pair of youse are in love, you'll be all right. You've
nothing to worry about in your mother nor me.'

I laugh and say: 'Doesn't news travel fast?'

'Faster than you'd think,' he says, and we walk on laughing and I'm so happy that I've come back here.

I get back to Athy on Sunday night. I sit in your kitchen
and put things in order in my mind. You have my photograph. I have your house. Your wife has nothing. I smile.

The summer passes. Every weekend I walk or cycle some
place. Sometimes with Noel, sometimes with girls from work,
sometimes on my own. I walk around Kilkea a lot. There and
in your house is where I find it easiest to be with you. I talk to
you all the time. I take plants from the fields and tell you
what they are. I point the differences between the spear thistle and the creeping thistle. This is the evening primrose and
this is the hawk's-beard. My father told me those. There are
places where I can talk to you and say things I may never say
to your face.

The summer ends and then the autumn.

I never wonder at his luck in being alive. I believe he will
never die. Always he has some stories in the post of death, of
bravery, of miracles.

'We went back to that village, to that café I wrote about.
The woman is still there. She hasn't changed. She hasn't

aged. She wore a brighter blouse this time. I took it as a sign. I have to laugh to think that someone like me, who never looked up from the ground, is seeing signs. And out here of all places. But I believe that nothing that has happened – no torn limb, no frantic horse, no soldier screaming, no shell that leaves me in an open grave with corpses all around – can come between us.

'The woman in the café lives, she dresses brightly, she smiles, I suppose she loves. All this a few miles from the front. She is the same as she was and so are you.'

'I have to write to tell you this. Today in the shop some women were talking about someone they'd heard was killed. One of them turned and said: "And how's your Frank?" I could have cried. "Your Frank." I laughed and said you were fine, that you'd be all right.

'And this woman said: "Of course he will, hasn't he you to come home to? Why wouldn't he be?" I think that was the happiest minute of my life. And you do have me. And I have you. And every night now I leave a space for you beside me and every morning I wake up in your space.'

The summer has passed and the autumn. Sometimes I wonder at my luck at being alive, at escaping without a scratch. Sometimes I am convinced I will never die.

His letters come. I find them on the windowsill in the hall when I get home from work. The envelope is always fat and full of paper, sometimes a dried flower that I put into a book

I keep. Sometimes I send a pressed flower back. But never one from his garden. Always wild flowers.

'Today is my birthday. I'm writing this in a garden or what remains of it. It's a garden on the edge of a town and it looks down across a valley. It's like looking out from the clear patch on the side of Mullaghcreelan, down across the castle and the houses in Kilkea. But here there's no village, just a clear valley of fields, without a tree. There's a river in the bed of the valley, as wide and cool as the Griese.

'I was here last spring when the place was paved with flowers. I prefer it now. It has the bite of home. We're billeted here but I've taken my blanket out into this garden to sleep. You get used to sleeping under the sky but here it's quiet. If the wind blows right, there isn't even a muffle of the guns.

'Lying under a tree at the end of the garden, I remember nights when we were out the Barrow line and, strange enough or maybe it isn't, I remember our last night. Our only night inside. My only regret is that the nights were too few and the distance seems so far. But not too far. This is the quietest, the happiest birthday of my life.

'I love you.'

I carried that letter to work with me and read it in the yard when things were quiet. I carried it home and that evening I went and sat in the room where we had lain and I read it and read it again. I wanted to write something like that but now, at such a distance from him, I could feel his passion flowing and mine was drowned.

161

'I've been thinking hard about things, now that I have the chance to. I thought maybe it was the great hate that made everything seem in its right place. But that can't be it because there's little or no hate here. None of us feels hate for who-ever is behind the big guns. We feel panic sometimes and we feel helpless for men that are dying in the dark, men we can hear shouting and can't reach, and we feel disgust at what the human body can look like, but we feel no hate. I've never felt as free of hate. I think it's the pain all around us that makes other feelings so important. That's what it is – the pain.

'Then the other feelings are more important than they were. You see a man get hit. You see the blood draining out of him the way we'd drain a lake. You see the life going with it. You look, when you have the time, and you see these things. You see a skin disappear and another one replacing it. You know the man is changing in a way you never get to understand but you recognise the change. It can happen as sudden as a dam bursting or it can be as slow as a summer evening. But you know death is coming on, it's like a mist. You see it and you don't. And you think about the other things that are draining out of this man. The love he wanted to talk about. And you realise there's no other time than the time we have now. You lie in a trench and as fast as anything you're somewhere else.

'I'm back with you on the haycocks out the Carlow road or in a field at Mullaghcreelan but this time I don't talk on and on. This time I kiss you and touch you and I forget the shells and the bullets and the mist that's always hanging over us.'

I read his letters. I keep them till I've finished my meal and then I take them across to his cottage and I read them in his room. I sit in his kitchen and write these letters in my head, letters I've been making up all day at work. Letters about the parts of me he barely touched. I write about the feelings and when he must do these things and how. But when it comes to writing the letters down, putting them on paper, they seem foolish. They never seem to have the ease of his.

And so I write: 'Everything here is as it was. Noel has all your apples in. They're laid out on the scullery floor on sheets of newspaper. The ones that weren't ripe are in the kitchen window. They catch whatever sun there is and I come and check on them in the evening.

'Noel laughs and says I should move in altogether and be done with it. The girls in work laugh, too, when I talk about you. "You're twenty-six," they say. "You'd better settle down. Get the house and then he'll have to take you!" I laugh at that. I think I'll wait. Do you want me to wait? Will it be as easy when you get back here?'

I ask the question more of myself than him but I am pleased when his answer comes in a torrent of words I wish he had used when he was here. His words explore each part of me.

'I want you to know these things. I came out here to take stock, to gather strength for going back. I have no fear of that. I don't care about the mouths that mouth. I care for our mouths and for the way they meet each other. For the way they meet strange parts of the body and don't find them strange at all.

'If a man here can be twisted, be hung from a stump or blown onto the top of a wall and left for days, he loses his life. We lose our respect for the unimportances. We put this aside and carry on surviving and when this war is over we'll put it aside and return to living.

'For me that means going back to the castle, cycling out in all weathers, working hard. It has nothing to do with what people say.

'For me it's getting back to the cottage. It has nothing to do with where the cottage is.

'For me it means my body and yours – the dry smell of your hair, the wet smell of me in you, the dark smell of the shadows your breasts make in the lamplight, the clean smell of us standing naked together wherever we want it to be. None of this worries me because I've been doing this for the last months, years, and so, I know, have you. We know each other's bodies. They will meet like friends and lovers who don't hesitate. They will find their way without more than the slightest touch to guide them.'

When I touch, my touch is of his hands.

'The thing I miss, apart from you, is trees. I'd love to climb a tree again and feel the particular way a tree is. There are no trees where we are now, only the occasional stump.

'I feel myself growing surer each week. I see men that we buried reappear. These are men without legs. Men whose heads are found elsewhere. I see men running, men I know to be dead. They go on running in the smoke, their faces dead. They fall eventually but by then the life is gone out of them. I see a man running on one leg. For a long time he thinks there are two and he goes on running perfectly. And then he

164

sees and he falls, crying, and we leave him there. We go on running because we have two legs under us and we want to keep them there.

'We rest against a parapet of flesh, of men gorged each into the next. I hate all these things – the shells, the gas, the buried and unburied dead – but it's the rain, puddled, dammed and trapped in trenches that hurts the most. It seeps in through the boots, through the ankles and the knees. Joints ache. Coats, soaked and muddy, dry and melt and dry again. Fresh shell holes smell of powder and then of rain. The water appears like holy wells around our feet. It comes from nowhere. We hear of thousands, hundreds of thousands, dying. We see them. We see the enemy from time to time but I hate only the rain.

'The lists go up on every side.

'We find a pair of legs, their owner is running somewhere, running on into the smoke.'

'My darling, I have read and read your letter until every page is tattered from turning and carrying. I don't care to leave it anywhere that someone might see it, so I bring it everywhere with me.

'When I read where you had written about me being your wife, I stopped. It was like a dream. Had I been asleep and missed out on that? I wondered. And then I realised what you were saying and that was even better. You say that since the night when we slept here I have been your wife. For me I have been your wife since very early on.

'And when you wrote all those things you think about, I knew exactly how you felt and I did what you asked. It was a sunny afternoon and I cycled out to the bridge at Kilkea and crossed the two fields and lay in that place where you asked me to and I knew you were there. It was the way you wrote it would be.

'When you come back that will be the first place we will go together. I love you more than everything and I often think that this war, this separation, was worth it after all because I know you're not gone.

'I love you, my darling. Mary Lloyd that now thinks of herself as Mary Kinsella.'

When we went forward we had blackened faces. It was night. We cut through wire. There were fewer flares than usual – a blessing. We came upon them suddenly, three young men, much younger than we were. They threw up their arms and we bayoneted them. Very little time to stop. We went through their uniforms. Then up and on across another no-man's-land. More muck, more sockets in the earth and legs and fingers pointing nowhere. Then up and on.

I thought I saw a level spray of bullets. I couldn't have but I thought I did. It started away to my left and neatly mowed through two of us. I was running, the other man was crouching. It tore my legs from just above the knees, it shot his head away. His lungs released a flow of air, a belch out through his open neck and he went down.

I thought of how the pain was less than I expected. I thought of how passion seemed less possible without my legs. I tried to picture her pushing me about in some stiff chair, lifting me like a bladder onto our bed. I was a different man and the future took on a different sense; it drained of any colour.

I had suspected this all along. I could look now and weigh the options for myself. And I could go on looking because by then I was dead. My body was half sitting, my open eyes stared straight ahead as my comrades raced by.

Of course the letter came to her. I could only laugh. And then they brought him home. She followed him along the street, between her brothers. He came in a box off the evening train, down past the shuttered windows and back again in the morning. Through the welcoming gates. She followed him and I followed to the top of the bridge and watched from there.

An army grave. She'd be buried with her own. I knew his grave was far too small. There was no crevice where I might knead my body between the earth and skin. I wished they'd left his bits in France. To have him lying at the head of the street while I pressed my naked self against the cold wet window as if he was there, out there, beyond it.

I set myself to live within the bounds that I had set myself. I turned myself on you but reaching back became a crime.

I have become content with naming things that marked our past, reverting to my former self: daffodil, wild violet, primrose, the cherry tree, bluebell, lilac, the golden rain, the marigold, the apple fruit, the rusting dahlias underneath.

His wife was there behind the hearse. One wife.

I saw no hope beyond the bounds that I had set myself and that is why I despise the angle now. I see the possibilities when they are gone.

167

If you can touch, then touch me now.

Daffodil, primrose, wild violet, the cherry tree, bluebell, lilac, the golden rain.

Across the street the laburnum bends, a kind of light.

The marigold, the apple fruit, the rusting dahlias underneath.

I press myself against the window and watch the ghostly dancers pass.

Frank Alcock.
Martin Hyland.
John Byrne.
Mick Lawlor.
Willie Tierney.
William Wall.
Owen Kelly.
Thomas Fox.
Stephen Mealy.
Joseph Hickey.
Larry Kelly.
Patrick Leonard.
Martin Moloney.
Robert MacWilliams.
Martin Maher.
Christopher Power.

Laurence Dooley.
Thomas Ellard.
Norman Hannon.
John Hannon.
Henry Hannon.
Thomas Hannon.
Frank Kinsella.
And Mary Lloyd.

I push my naked body through the glass and join the dismal
dead who pass.